Harlequin
Presents..

VIOLET WINSPEAR

love's prisoner

HARLEQUIN BOOKS
toronto-winnipeg

© Violet Winspear 1964

Original hard cover edition published in 1964
by Mills & Boon Limited

SBN 373-70536-0
Harlequin Presents edition published February 1974

Printed in Canada.

CHAPTER ONE

THE sitting-room of the Ellis house was in darkness but for the flickering of the fire. A mellow voice crooned of love from the record-player, while Eden Ellis lay curled among the cushions of the chintz-covered settee.

Eden hummed a few bars of the song, and then broke into a slight smile at the way Aunt Sue had ordered Uncle Harry to take her out tonight. 'I refuse to be here when that Sheridan man calls for Gale,' she had said. 'She's deliberately encouraging a man whose way of life is totally different from ours ... a man none of us could possibly like or feel at ease with.'

This didactic view of the situation had grated on Uncle Harry's sense of fair play. 'Now, Sue,' he had reproved her, 'I can't say I entirely approve of this—er—friendship which Gale has struck up with Lafe Sheridan, but I don't agree with condemning him out of hand. Certainly not for your reasons, my dear!'

Aunt Sue had stared through the wall mirror at her husband, one hand holding a small hat to her head, the other clenching a long, dangerous-looking pin. 'What do you mean by that remark, Harry?' She had looked unusually fierce.

'He isn't like any of the other young men who've come to the house, is he, Sue? He worries you because he isn't an artless young local with nothing more serious on his mind than tennis, dancing, and swimming. He's a tough business executive, and he can no more help looking like one than I can help looking like the district manager of an insurance office. Neither can he help the fact that nature built him higher and wider than the usual run of men.'

A shrewd thrust, in Eden's opinion. Lafe Sheridan had about him a very positive maleness.

'He's been around, Harry,' her aunt had obstinately argued. 'No man of thirty-seven gets to look that hard-bitten unless he's lived a full life, and that's why I don't want a niece of mine to get mixed up with him. There's no knowing where he'll take her! He probably frequents those night-clubs where all manner of things go on!'

'They come off, Sue!' Uncle Harry had laughed. 'Anyway, Gale is over twenty-one and quite capable of taking care of herself—but I'm not saying we wouldn't have something to worry about if it was our young Eden he was taking out.'

Eden's smile grew rueful as she popped a chocolate into her mouth. What a nuisance to be only nineteen and the owner of looks that seemed to give people the impression that she had not yet fathomed the mystery of the birds and the bees...

At that moment the doorbell pealed and Eden

uncurled her slim legs and darted to the window. She jerked aside the curtain, but no long, gleaming car stood in front of the house, and when she reached the front door and opened it, she found Tony Gregg on the doorstep ... he was a friend of her sister's.

'Hullo, Paradise!'

Eden usually greeted her schoolgirl nickname with a resigned smile, but tonight her eyes held a worried expression as she let Tony into the house.

'Is Gale in?' he wanted to know.

'She's—getting ready to go out, Tony.'

Eden flicked on the sitting-room light and he trailed behind her to the fireplace. 'Who is it tonight—anyone I know?' A note of jealousy roughened his voice.

Eden took hold of the poker and prodded the coals in a nervously angry way. Love robbed people of their pride, she thought. It made puppets of them. Danced them on strings, threw them down and hurt them, then made them dance attendance again. She wanted to say to Tony, 'Why do you let Gale hurt you, over and over? There are other girls in Lowton, less pretty, perhaps, but not so ambitious as Gale.'

She switched off the record-player and tried to sound casual as she told him about Lafe Sheridan.

'You've got to be kidding, Eden.' Tony looked stunned. 'How would Gale come to meet a man like that in Lowton? He's the boss of one of the biggest citrus firms in the world!'

'I know.' Eden perched on the arm of a chair. 'I was the one who first met him.'

'*You*, Eden?'

'It happened the other evening.' She fingered the accordion pleats of her skirt. 'It was snowing when I left off work, and I was crossing the High Street when a car belted round from the heath. I dashed for the kerb, but before I could get there I slid over on a patch of ice. The car screeched to a halt only a yard away, a man leapt out of it and hoisted me off the ground in his arms. I was still a bit stunned, but that didn't stop me from recognizing him. I had seen him as a guest on that television programme, *Dinner Talk*, and it gave me the strangest feeling to—well, look in his eyes, and be told off by him for wandering across main roads in a daydream.

'He,' she added indignantly, 'was driving his monster of a car as though he thought Lowton's main road a racing track!'

'Typical bit of arrogance of the self-made man,' Tony growled. 'I suppose he then turned all gallant and gave you a lift home?'

'He came in for a cup of coffee.'

'And met Gale?'

Eden gave a slight shrug, for to meet her sister Gale was to be enchanted, and Lafe Sheridan was very much a man.

Lafe, she informed Tony, was taking Gale to

8

dinner and a show in nearby Brighton. He was staying there at a hotel while he negotiated the purchase of a house on the Downs. It was a large house, a bit run down at the moment, but he planned to restore it to its former beauty and to add a swimming-pool.

'He's rich as Midas, eh?' Tony's hand shook slightly as he lit himself a cigarette. His blue-grey eyes were hurt and angry. 'Well off, with a big ornate car. Suits from Whitley's and a champagne smile. And what am I? Junior partner in a country medical practice. Suits from Duff's in the High Street, and an old Ford with a bent fender!'

Tony paced the hearthrug, a slender young man, with a bony, intelligent face and a strip of fair moustache across his upper lip. His hair had a Nordic brightness under the electric light, and Eden could well understand why Aunt Sue always called him nice and open and dependable. The best of qualities, but dispensable as far as Gale was concerned.

'I've carried a torch for Gale since you both came to live here when your parents died.' He took a long pull at his cigarette. 'I can't help the way I feel about her, even though she goes her own way and fibs to me when it suits her. I saw her in town yesterday, but she said nothing about this Sheridan chap.'

He flicked ash into the fireplace, and quizzed Eden's intent young face. 'Maybe I shouldn't be talking like this to you, Eden, but there's no one else I can say it to, and it all boils up in a man—up to here!' He touched his throat and his eyes were stormy. 'I'd do a lot for Gale, almost anything, but I can't leave Lowton. She doesn't care that my father made sacrifices so I could go through medical college and come home here to be his partner—but I care, Eden. I—I can't walk out on him, especially since Ma died—not even for Gale.'

'No, don't walk out on your father, Tony. You're right to stick by him, and Gale's very wrong to ask you to do otherwise.' Eden's hands clenched together. 'She uses her beauty like a weapon at times.'

He nodded, even as he looked surprised. Eden was just a kid, but there were times when she seemed to possess a wisdom beyond her years—a wisdom that made Gale's worldliness seem shallow by comparison. 'Do you like this Sheridan man, Eden?' he asked.

'Does it matter what I think of the men whom Gale chooses to go out with?' Her gaze was as if held by the fire.

'I value your opinion, Eden. You've got a lot of sense, for a kid.'

'I'm not a kid,' she said indignantly. 'All of you are a little too fond of thinking I'm still in my school uniform with my hair in a plait down my back. I discarded both a couple of years ago.'

Tony gave a grin and studied her through his

cigarette smoke. Her elfin-styled hair was feathered with tawny highlights, her straight small nose and thin cheeks were faintly freckled. She possessed a sort of woodland charm. 'Come on, Eden, you must have formed some sort of an opinion of Sheridan of the famous Soft Drinks and Ales.'

She interlaced her slim fingers and thought of Lafe in the snow, his dark hair glistening with it, his arms holding her without effort, his green eyes curiously magnetic ... and yet lonely.

His eyes had told her why the newpaper-men dubbed him 'the lonely tycoon'.

Somehow it suited Lafe Sheridan, the Irish orphan lad who had sailed to foreign parts to make his fortune. Out in South Africa the tough life of a diamond miner had absorbed him until he had drifted into part-ownership of a run-down fruit farm. Driven relentlessly by his memories of a loveless, hungry boyhood, he had worked to build up the farm, and then he had branched out into the business of producing citrus drinks, and a tangy golden ale that had become famous all over the globe.

He once again proved to the world that rags to riches was a possibility, but the stories that circulated about him were curiously impersonal. He was one of the shrewdest, most feared financiers, and he was still under forty, yet little was known about his private life. Men admired his capability for making money ... women were attracted to his wealth *and* his ruthless dark looks, but so far 'the lonely tycoon' had not turned his steps in the direction of the altar.

'He's a man with a great deal of power,' Eden said thoughtfully. 'Yet I don't think he's entirely— happy. He has possessions, but they aren't enough, are they?'

'*We* know they aren't,' Tony agreed quietly.

Eden's glance rested on Tony's fair-skinned face, so different from Lafe's dark, forceful one, the left cheek furrowed by a slash of cynicism when he smiled.

'You can't blame him for wanting Gale's company for an evening.' Eden smiled. 'She can be such good fun.'

'He may want more than a night out!' Tony looked morose. 'He may fall in love with her.'

'Yes,' Eden had to agree. 'He's lonely, and Gale's lovely. When you're lonely, love is rather like a 'flu germ diving into a body which is a bit under the weather. You're infected before you know where you are.'

'You make love sound like an uncomfortable infection, Eden.' Tony half smiled. 'Anyway, what would a kid like you know about love?'

'I—I can imagine what it's like.' She flushed slightly.

'Have you been holding out on everyone?' Tony regarded the colour in her cheeks with amused eyes. 'Has a clerk down at the Welfare Centre swept you off your feet?'

'Heavens, no!'

'Don't they make passes at you, Paradise?'

'I don't want them to, thanks. They're a stuffy bunch of males in bowler hats.'

Tony chuckled. 'You look fetching, Paradise, when you flash those big brown eyes.'

'Like a spaniel,' she grinned.

'As a matter of fact,' he stared openly at her, 'you're rather like Gale—I've never noticed it before.'

Eden touched a hand to her cheek and felt its thin young curve. 'I—I've never given it a thought that we might be a little alike. Gale's so vivid and striking.'

'You're the subtle one.' Tony gave her hair a tweak. 'The pair of you are as different as wine and water.'

'I'm the water, I suppose?'

'Yes, the pure aqua, clear and refreshing. Gale goes to the head like ... oh, to the devil with her!' He tossed his cigarette butt into the fire with a tormented motion of his head. 'I'd better be on my way before the Ale King gets here.'

But he had left it too late.

A couple of long peals on the doorbell echoed through the house, and Eden avoided looking at Tony as she went to answer the door. She was half-way along the narrow hall when a rustle of silk made her glance up the stairs.

Gale stood at the head of the stairs, breathtaking in a rose brocade dress borrowed from the shop where she worked as a combined saleslady and model. The dress was low-cut, with fascinating bell-sleeves to just below the elbows. The full skirt emphasized the trimness of Gale's waist, and she seemed to Eden to have just stepped out of a picture frame.

'Let him in!' She stood regal and lovely there on the landing, ready to intoxicate Lafe's senses when he walked in through the door. For a fleeting moment Eden almost disliked her sister for the deliberate way she was setting out to trap Lafe, and for the uncaring manner in which she trampled on Tony Gregg's feelings.

Eden jerked open the front door. 'Good evening, Mr. Sheridan!' She stood rather tensely to one side, so that he might see only Gale as he stepped into the house. But he was staring at Eden. She didn't know it, but she had gone rather white.

'Hullo!' His voice was deep and still very Irish. 'What's up with you?'

She gazed back at him speechlessly.

'You look a bit frail. Have you been putting in more overtime down at that Welfare Centre where you work?'

'We're rather busy at present—and I can always make use of the extra money.'

'*You* can?' He quirked an eyebrow, and then turned deliberately to gaze at Gale as she came down the stairs, her rose brocade skirts whispering and flouncing and her fur wrap trailing the carpet behind her, for all the world as if she had a dozen furs and had not borrowed from Eden to pay the instalments. Gale never had a penny left out of her own earning.

'It's customary for one's escort to say something complimentary.' Gale's voice was huskily attractive, and her topaz eyes were taking in the superb tailoring of her escort's overcoat, dark vicuña, the collar thrust up about his dark-tanned neck and face. 'Do you find me good to look at, Lafe?'

'Are there words to describe the way you look?' His left cheek flaunted its slashing cleft as he handed her a box with a cellophane lid. 'A rough diamond like myself pays his compliments with orchids.'

'Orchids, Lafe?' Gale's eyes grew lustrous with pleasure as she accepted the box and went rustling into the sitting-room. Eden walked into the room ahead of Lafe, and she watched her sister open the box and take out of it a pair of exotic, gold-splashed green orchids. She gave a thrilled laugh. 'They're gorgeous, Lafe!'

'You look gorgeous yourself,' Tony murmured.

Gale whirled round, noticing him for the first time. 'I—I didn't know you were here!' Then she recovered her composure, laughed and threw out a hand in Tony's direction. 'This is one of Eden's boy-friends, Lafe. His name is Tony Gregg. Now tell me, shall I put my orchids just here?' She held them to her waist and when he nodded she pinned them to the brocade, uncaring that the gown was not really hers to mar.

'There!' The orchids caressed Gale's waist, her shoulders and her throat rose creamy-skinned out of the rose brocade, her eyes were golden on Lafe Sheridan's face.

Eden could feel the hard thumping of her heart. How cruel of Gale to dismiss Tony in that cool, disparaging voice! How dared she call him one of *her* boy-friends! Poor Tony looked as hurt as though Gale had struck him across the face!

'Do you like my gown, Eden—Tony?' Gale paraded back and forth and the brocade shimmered and emitted the perfume she had sprayed on—twenty-seven shillings an ounce, she had told Eden!

'She smells nice, doesn't she, Paradise?' With a faintly reckless laugh Tony drew Eden into the circle of his arm.

'Don't they make a charming couple?' Gale preened in front of the mirror, while Lafe cast his glacial green glance over the fair-haired young man with his arm around Eden.

A cold tremor ran through her and she wondered at Gale's audacity, the way she could plunge them into deceit and go on looking as untroubled as a child who hadn't yet learned the difference between right and wrong.

'This pantomime's a little out of gear,' Tony remarked. 'We've got a Cinderella—Gale, of course. We've a Prince Charming and I'm Buttons, but where does Paradise fit into all this?' He slanted a grin down at Eden. 'Who are you supposed to be? You're certainly not one of the Ugly Sisters.'

'Eden is my Good Fairy.' Gale strolled to Lafe in her golden dancing shoes and twined an arm about his dark-clad one. 'It was she who waved a wand and produced Prince Charming for me.'

Lafe was looking sardonic as he met her golden eyes. 'If I remember correctly, Cinderella was rather shy.'

'Oh, things have changed since those days,' Gale said pertly. 'Nowadays Cinderella knows what she wants and she doesn't rely on losing her glass slipper.'

'What a pity,' drawled Lafe. 'That was always the most charming part of the story.'

'I can't believe that *you* enjoy fables,' Gale scoffed.

'Can't *you?*' He quirked a black eyebrow above glinting green eyes. 'I'm Irish, remember. We're steeped in the belief that pixies come out at night and lead us astray.'

Even as Gale laughed, Eden felt the flick of green eyes, taking in her elfin-cut hair and her wand of a body. Because of this she edged closer to Tony, who didn't mock at everything as Lafe

17

Sheridan seemed to.

Gale stood slender in front of Lafe as he adjusted her fur wrap about her bare shoulders. 'Are you aware, you lovely witch,' he half laughed, 'that there's ice on the hedges tonight?'

She slanted a provocative smile up into his face. 'You've a heater in your car, haven't you?'

Eden slipped out of Tony's encircling arm, and she was plumping the settee cushions when Lafe said to her: 'Goodnight—Paradise.'

She glanced up, in the grip of an unnatural anger. 'Don't call me that! It's a silly name—I've long outgrown it.'

'Mr. Gregg doesn't seem to think so.' He gave her that sardonic, rather foreign bow of his. His nod of goodnight to Tony was rather curt, then he and Gale walked out to his car, and Gale's excited laughter came trilling back to them.

Gale was glowing with triumph when she told Eden all about the dinner and show the following evening.

'I had a fabulous time,' she enthused. 'I sat among men who smoked expensive cigars and next to women with sables thrown round them with all the negligence we would throw on a raincoat. I enjoyed delicious food in an exclusive restaurant and was hovered over by the waiters as if I were a princess!'

Gale's eyes were golden with pleasure, but she

18

made no mention of the man who had made her pleasure possible.

'It was more than fun, Eden,' she said. 'It was as though I'd never lived before, and it isn't living in my opinion unless you have money ... lots of it. You're looked up to when you have it, you're just average when you haven't. It's even a waste of time to be good-looking if you can't show yourself off in the smartest places, dressed in the right kind of clothes.

'Eden,' Gale hugged herself, 'I saw men look at me last night as if they thought me really beautiful, and the intoxication of it went to my head like the champagne we had to drink.'

Eden couldn't help but smile at this burst of girlish joy from her sister. For someone as attractive as Gale, perhaps it was understandable that she should want gorgeous clothes and admiration.

But along with these, didn't she want love? Didn't Lafe want it?

Gale studied her young sister's mind and seemed, shrewdly, to read her mind. 'Lafe, my pet, wants an entertaining hostess for that big house he's buying. He wants a beautiful toy he can dress up, show off, and amuse himself with. Being Lafe Sheridan's toy might have its moments—in more ways than the purely financial.'

Gale's lovely mouth curved into a meaning smile, and she admired her slim left hand as if already she visualized a fabulous ring upon it.

Eden wandered to the record-player, where she stood sorting through the long-players. She selected one and placed it on the turntable, and as music from *The King And I* drifted into the room, Gale came over and put her arms around Eden's waist. 'You're a bit old-fashioned, aren't you, darling?' she laughed. 'What's the matter? Does Lafe alarm you?'

'Why should he?' Eden asked. 'He thinks I'm a schoolgirl and treats me accordingly.'

'I don't think you're very smitten with him,' Gale persisted, amusedly. 'He is rather larger than life, isn't he? A black Irishman—they're said to make fierce enemies, so be careful not to let him guess how you feel about him, kitten.'

Eden tensed at these words. 'I can feel you trembling,' her sister accused. 'My pet, he won't gobble me up in those strong white teeth of his. He's really quite human when you get to know him—he even likes to dance.'

'Tea is ready, girls.' Their aunt came bustling into the sitting-room. 'Now don't let it stand and get cold. You've the rest of the evening in which to talk about dancing.'

Eden silently blessed the interruption and slipped free of her sister's hands.

She didn't have to be told that Lafe was human and therefore vulnerable, as likely to be bowled over by Gale's amazing attraction as other men had been. In the snow with him, Eden had caught a glimpse of someone who was very solitary ... who needed to be loved for himself.

Gale was in love with all the material things he could give her. Lovely clothes, trips abroad, and being the centre of attention as the wife of an important man. She was so bedazzled by the thought of these that she was ready to pretend to feelings she didn't feel at all. A dangerous ... emotional situation.

CHAPTER TWO ·

GALE had been to a race-meeting with Lafe the afternoon they brought Gareth Conway to the Ellis house for the first time.

Gareth was in his early twenties, a talented pianist with a very promising musical career ahead of him, thanks to Lafe. He had taken the boy under his wing when, out in Africa, Gareth's widower father had died following a tree-felling accident.

Gareth had been a teenage boy at the time, and he later confided to Eden that he owed everything to Lafe's generosity—a sound education, then the opportunity to accept a musical scholarship. His sincere appreciation of all his guardian had done for him was at the root of the friendship which quickly flowered between Eden and the young pianist.

His lean frame, his slow way of smiling that crinkled his sorrel eyes beneath unruly hair, held an appeal for Aunt Sue. She made him welcome in her house without any of the reserve which showed in her manner towards Lafe. The Irish tycoon was very open-handed, she admitted to Eden, and he seemed to get pleasure out of giving Gale the social whirl she had always craved. He had even put some insurance in Harry's way which had not come amiss, but still she found him an alarming sort of man ... especially when he stood a dark giant among the flowered chintzes and china knick-knacks of her sitting-room.

She frankly told Eden one evening what a relief it was to her that he had chosen to come courting her slightly older, more worldly-wise niece. 'He met you first, Eden, and neither your uncle nor I would have stood for him calling on you.'

'I'm hardly Lafe's type.' Eden's elfin head was bent over a book.

'That's true, my dear.' Aunt Sue ran a comfortable glance over the blouse she was making for Eden. 'But I know someone else who thinks you his type.'

'Do you, Aunt Sue?' Eden couldn't resist teasing her aunt with a look of puzzlement. 'Now who on earth can you mean?'

'You know very well who I'm talking about, my girl. Gareth's a charming boy, and you wouldn't go out with him if you didn't think so yourself. Thank heaven your poor dear parents didn't leave me two flirtatious nieces to cope with!'

Gale's tendency to like the admiration of the opposite sex had always been a source of worry to Aunt Sue. 'She's so exciting to look at,' Eden smiled. 'She attracts men without being able to help herself.'

'Mmm, and not always the type I approve of,'

grumbled Aunt Sue. 'Now if only she would settle down with Tony—he's such a nice, dependable boy, and his family have always lived in Lowton. We know the Greggs, whereas—well, what do we know about Lafe Sheridan beyond the fact that he's wealthy?'

'He's worked very hard to make his money,' Eden pointed out, 'and he treats Gareth like a son. One of the reasons he has bought a house in England is because he wants Gareth to start his career over here.'

'Yes, he's good to Gareth,' Aunt Sue conceded. 'All the same I do find him disconcerting. The way he smiles, for instance! Now you must admit, Eden, that he has a—a devilish sort of smile. One can never tell what's behind it.'

'He's cynical,' Eden admitted. 'But that's sometimes a cover-up for—deeper feelings. A sort of armour to protect himself.'

'*Humph.*' Aunt Sue was not to be converted to the idea that Lafe Sheridan needed any sort of protection. 'He's hard as rock, and it's Gale who needs to take care. She may think herself capable of twisting any man round her finger, but she'll hit a snag if she tries it on with that man. He's leading *her*, and parties and the flowers are the bait.'

'Lafe isn't that sort,' Eden exclaimed. 'He isn't out to seduce Gale!'

'No,' Aunt Sue agreed quietly. 'I think he's out to marry her, and the very thought makes me unhappy—for both of them. He's shrewd enough to know that she's avaricious. But is she shrewd enough to know that once married he'll permit no compromise? He'll give her lovely clothes and jewellery, but he'll demand his own dues. He'll be a husband in every sense of the word—and it will be too late for that silly girl to turn to Tony.'

Eden's eyes widened. 'Then you think——?'

'I think if Lafe Sheridan had never come into our lives, Eden, your sister would eventually have married Tony Gregg. He's the one she has never quite discarded from her wide circle of male admirers. He's the one she runs to when she feels unhappy. Haven't you noticed, my dear?'

Eden nodded, and a pensive silence fell between them. Uncle Harry broke it when he came in from his study, rubbing his hands and saying it was cold in there and that he felt ready for a nice hot cup of coffee.

Lafe bought his house on the Downs, and now the interior restoration was completed he and Gareth moved in. Workmen were still busy laying the tiles of the swimming-pool—green as Lafe's eyes, according to Gale—and Gareth drove Eden up to see the house on a Sunday afternoon in April.

His rakish sports car turned off a road through the hills and sped along a rural lane whose hedges frothed with a wild purple flower. Eden's hair was tossed by a fresh and scented breeze, and she wore a cherry-red suit, and felt a bitter-sweet eagerness to see Lafe's house.

'Lafe's a darn good sort,' Gareth said warmly. 'He's given me my own special music-room, and even had it sound-proofed so I can work on my music without being disturbed. I'll never be able to pay him back for all he's done for me, Eden.'

'I imagine he feels repaid each time he hears you play the piano, Gareth.' Eden's glance dwelt on the slender hands on the wheel of the car, so different from the large brown hands that had driven her home in the snow. 'It must give him a great deal of satisfaction to know he's fostered a talent like yours.'

'I often think Lafe gives me the things he would have liked himself at my age,' Gareth said thoughtfully. 'He has a terrific brain and he'd have revelled in a college education, the chance of choosing a career instead of being pitchforked on to the battlefield of big business. It's scarred him, Eden. Made him a lot harder and cynical than I believe he was meant to be. His deprived boyhood made him want the security of money, but along the way he's collected a lot of disillusionment about people.'

Eden knew that Gareth meant women. Women in all the big capitals of the world, clamouring for Lafe's attention and his gifts, and never asking if he had a heart to share.

Gareth's car swung into a driveway, with trees arching overhead for about half a mile, then another turn of the wheel brought them to the steps of the Tudor house.

Bellevue, drowsing in April sunshine, a half-timbered, black and white dream of a house, its diamond-leaded windows peering through the arching branches of a golden elm. A cloud of fragrant wistaria rose to meet the tawny, beetling thatch of the long roof.

'I think that thatching reminded him of the veld,' Gareth smiled. 'His place out in Africa has a massive thatched roof and a great deep porch, shaded by a veranda and tiled with red stones. This house is smaller, but it's got charm, eh?'

Eden had no words to express her delight in Bellevue. It blended into the downy landscape, a hideaway for a busy man, a blessed retreat from the cares of big business.

Lafe was in London today on business, so Gareth played master and conducted Eden on a tour of the rooms, in which the patina of well-chosen furniture blended warmly with the rich colours of the brocade drapes and the pile carpets. The rooms were soothing rather than splendid, and it was only here and there that Lafe's wealth showed itself in a flash of opulence.

They had tea in Gareth's music-room, where Eden sat in one of the deep window-seats while Gareth sat at the piano and played his latest composition. His touch on the keys was a caress, and Eden listened dreamily and gazed out across the rolling downland, dappled with sheep and their spring-born lambs. The sky was turning to a hazy pink. Dusk was creeping across the downs.

When the music faded, a magical hush prevailed.

'Well, Eden?' Gareth murmured.

She turned with a soft awakening sigh to look at him across the room. 'What have you called it?' she asked softly.

'*Woodland Nymph*.' He smiled and pushed an unruly lock of hair from his right eye. 'You inspired it.'

Eden caught her breath, then with a pleased laugh she ran to him and gave him a hug. 'I love it, and I'm very flattered to think I inspired you to write it.'

'Deserves more than a hug, don't you think?' His smile was half shy, half coaxing, and suddenly he pulled her down beside him on the piano bench and held her there.

'I suppose I'm your prisoner until I give you a kiss?' She brushed her lips across his cheek, and his hold was tightening on her when the door of the music-room opened. A tall figure stepped into the room, and the two young people, their heads close together, were silhouetted against the pinky dusk-light.

'Mr. Sheridan!' Eden jumped up from the piano bench.

'Hullo, Lafe!' Gareth reached to the piano lamp and switched it on. 'I thought you were staying up in London until Tuesday?'

'I came home for some factory data we'll need at the board meeting tomorrow. I'm driving back again tonight.'

'The mere thought of your energy makes me feel exhausted,' Gareth grinned. 'It's a wonder you don't crack up, Lafe.'

'I'm too tough for that.' Lafe flicked a glance over Eden's white blouse and cherry-red skirt, dwelt longer on the tinge of pink beneath her freckles. 'What do you think of Bellevue, pixie?'

'It's a charming house,' she replied guardedly.

'That, Lafe, is the understatement of the year,' Gareth scoffed. 'Eden has fallen headlong for your house. Her eyes were glistening like pools of tawny sherry while I was showing her over it.'

Lafe quirked an eyebrow and smiled. 'I shall have to think about a house-warming party directly the pool is finished and the workmen have trundled their gear away. Mmm, Gale can enjoy herself arranging the do—tell me, Eden, do you like parties?'

'The parties Gale arranges are always fun.' She leaned against the glossy darkness of the piano, her blouse and skirt throwing into relief the slenderness of her body. Lafe overtopped her by more than a foot, and as always she felt his dark vitality like a bludgeon. She almost wanted to keel over under it. . . .

The cool clear green of his eyes was intensified by the denseness of his lashes as he suggested that she stay to dinner if her aunt wasn't expecting her home. He could drop her off at the house on his way back to London.

'Yes, stay to dinner with a pair of lonely bachelors,' Gareth coaxed.

Twilight had dropped its mantle down over Bellevue, and Eden knew herself bewitched, unable yet to tear herself away from this Tudor hideaway on the downs. With a smile she accepted the invitation, and the three of them made their way downstairs.

They had dinner by candlelight in the Tudor dining-room, and Lafe suggested that they enjoy their coffee in the lounge. The ruby-red curtains had been drawn, tiny blue flames curled over the logs in the big stonework fireplace, and Eden felt lost in the huge embrace of a wing-back chair. A manservant poured coffee and handed it round, then he quietly withdrew, and as Eden stirred her coffee she wondered if Lafe harped back very often in his mind to his orphan boyhood in Ireland.

She watched as he poured liqueurs into stemmed glasses, and thought of what Uncle Harry had said about the gambling streak that was part of the character of the financial wizard. There was in that strong Irish face, she decided, a dash of recklessness that warred with the firm moulding of the chin and the aggressive jut of the nose. It was there in his mouth ... a bold mouth that held her gaze as she accepted her liqueur from his fingers.

'Thank you, Mr. Sheridan,' she murmured.

'Too shy to call me Lafe?' he asked mockingly. 'Surely we're friends by now?'

'Very well—Lafe.'

'That's much friendlier.' He smiled and with an habitual jerk at the knife-edge creases of his trousers sat down in a winged chair and rested his dark head against the ribbed red velvet. 'When the pool's ready for use, you must stay a weekend and make use of it, with Gareth. I'm having a tennis-court laid out as well—you don't belong to the Sports Club like Gale, do you?'

'Nor to the Drama Society,' she smiled. 'I'm the solitary type.'

'H'm,' he cast a thoughtful glance at Gareth, then requested a little music to get him in a serene mood for his drive back to London.

Gareth sat down at the lounge piano, which had a rosewood frame and was of a lighter build than the Bechstein up in his music-room. He drifted into the piece of music he had composed himself and called *Woodland Nymph*.

Eden's thick lashes shielded her eyes as she watched Lafe in the opposite chair. He was smoking a cigar and listening with relaxed ease to the enchanting melody stealing out from beneath Gareth's talented fingers. When the music faded away he nodded to himself, as if to say that all he had done for Gareth had paid off, with dividends. 'I like that piece very much,' he said to his ward. 'Have you given it a name?'

Gareth told him the name of the piece, and Eden caught the speculation in Lafe's glance at herself. At her curled-up legs in the big chair, her elfin hair and freckled nose. There was a smile on the edge of his mouth as he rose to his feet and said it was time they were making a move. He held out a hand to her and she took it and uncurled to her feet with the slim silent grace of a little cat. The liquéur and the music had given her eyes a drowsy look.

'I'll get those papers I came for, and see you out by the car—nymph.'

Gareth fetched her jacket from the music-room and escorted her to Lafe's car, which gleamed darkly in the pale light of a slender moon. The touch of Gareth's hands on her waist was rather more possessive than she had yet known them. 'I've tickets for a show on Wednesday evening,' he murmured. 'Will you come with me?'

'If you'd like me to.'

'You know I'd like you with me all the time!' His warm lips brushed her temple, she felt a tremor course through him and was wrapped suddenly in his arms. She tensed with the awareness that at any moment Lafe would stride in from the house and see them.

'Gareth, please!' She fought to escape from his arms, and he laughed at her inability to do so.

'Lafe knows how it is with us, darling, so stop struggling like a butterfly in a net.'

'Lafe knows—what do you mean?' Her eyes lifted rather wildly to Gareth's face.

'He's guessed how we feel about each other. Didn't you see the way he looked at us in the lounge? I know that half smile of his. I know when he's pleased....'

Eden hardly felt Gareth's mouth on her own; she barely realized that he was kissing her.

'Don't be all night over that, Gareth,' drawled a sardonic voice.

Eden tore herself out of Gareth's arms, muttered goodnight and slipped into Lafe's car. He entered through the driver's door, tossed a briefcase to the back seat and the next moment was swinging the big car away from the house. He drove silently and swiftly, and it wasn't until they passed below Ditchling Beacon that he commented on the singular stillness and peace of the moonlit downs.

'I particularly like this part of England,' he said. 'Here, as in Africa, the stars seem to glimmer on the hilltops.'

She detected a note of nostalgia in his voice, and guessed that he had grown to think of South Africa as his home. 'Will you be staying long in England?' she asked.

'I shall stay to see the new factory started,' he

replied. 'But my temperament is a restless one and I like the African climate. Then again the bulk of my business is conducted out there. It doesn't do for the Big Boss to be absent too long.'

She smiled at the description, and could imagine the glossy, coal-dark Africans referring to him as Big Boss. There was much about him that was intimidating, yet she felt certain he was a popular employer. He too had sweated in the hot sun for a wage. He knew what it felt like to have blistered hands and aching shoulders.

'Does it strike you as strange that I should choose to buy a house in England rather than Ireland?' he remarked.

'Not really—Lafe.' Her eyes dwelt on the forceful structure of his sun-darkened profile. 'Why should you deliberately choose to be reminded of past misery?'

'Why indeed!' The rough velvet of his voice seemed to rasp her skin for a moment. 'Bellevue is quite a place, eh? Well worth the money it took to restore the panelling and the thatched roof. I've a weakness for those beetling roofs.'

'Gareth told me about your place in South Africa. It must be very colourful.' As she spoke Eden wondered what Gale's reaction would be when she learned that Lafe meant to return to Africa. Eden knew her sister had visions of visiting Rome, loafing in the sunshine of Corfu, living it up under the bright lights of Paris.

Lafe's home in South Africa was probably in the wilds, for his money had not robbed him of an inborn love of solitude. He would, Eden thought, have to be desperately in love before he subordinated his wishes to those of a woman ... and then again the woman who truly loved him would revel in his mastery.

Suddenly he stopped the car at the very height of the Downs and they took in together the moonlight in its folds and hollows, and the many stars that gemmed the sky. 'Makes one feel humble ... almost enough to throw off worldly cares and to say to the devil with strife.'

Eden glanced at Lafe, and it seemed to her that the soft lighting of the car's interior etched his mouth into lines of appeal, and something of pain.

'Aren't you free to do exactly as you want?' she asked.

'There are too many commitments, Eden. I hold the leading reins of Sheridan's and I daren't let go of them. It isn't arrogance—it's just my particular tiger and I've got to keep riding him.'

'People's jobs are involved, aren't they, Lafe?'

'Yes. It's Africa and there are problems. But a youngster like yourself doesn't want to hear about that.' He rested an arm on the wheel and studied her face in the soft lighting. 'That tumble in the snow was lucky for both of us, eh? You met Gareth. I met Gale.'

She nodded and he started up the car. They said

goodnight at the gate of the Ellis house and he told her to tell Gale he'd be giving her a ring from London. He meant he'd be telephoning her sister, but the word conjured up another image in Eden's mind. She sensed, as the car drove off, that Lafe meant to propose to Gale in the near future.

The next few days turned out to be trying ones at the Welfare Centre. Eden was secretary to the welfare officer in charge of hardship relief for the town's old people, and a new building plan was going to cause upheaval for the occupants of some old-world cottages. Eden had to go round with the welfare officer, and it was a hurting business to see the faces of the cottagers when they were told that their homes were due for demolition and that they were going to be moved into bed-sitter flats in Redford.

The flats had window-boxes, but no gardens, no trellised porches for sitting beneath on a starlit night, with the roses in bloom, bringing back memories.

'They're such pretty cottages,' Eden sighed. 'Do they have to be pulled down?'

'I'm afraid this is the age of progress.' The welfare officer shrugged his shoulders. 'Sentiment can't be allowed to stand in its way.'

'Ignore sentiment and you gradually stamp out humanity.' Eden's eyes were concerned and anxious as she thought of the bewilderment on old

Sam Carstairs' seamed face, the reproach that replaced Rosie Barrat's broad smile.

'Gradually all the beauty will be drained out of England and we'll be left with nothing but boxlike houses and flats. And another sad aspect is the fact that those old people are not going to be allowed to keep their pets. Mrs. Barrat will break her heart if she has to have Marmalade put to sleep. The cat's a beautiful creature. Rosie's son gave him to her before he left for Aden, where he died in a street battle. He was a soldier.'

'We're providing these people with the best sort of accommodation available ... you've seen these flatlets, Miss Ellis. They're really much more wholesome and convenient than those tumbledown cottages.'

'The council could add a few amenities and let them stand,' Eden argued.

'You are a dreamer, I fear, Miss Ellis.'

'I fear I am,' Eden agreed.

A fortnight later Lafe decided to have his housewarming party, and the arrangements were left entirely to a glowing and eager Gale. By now she had met quite a few of Lafe's business friends and social acquaintances and the guest list was quite a long one, with one or two titled names to enhance it. She invited several of her own friends, but coolly excluded all relatives but Eden and her aunt and uncle.

Aunt Sue was indignant about this and accused

Gale of being a snob.

'I'm nothing of the sort,' Gale denied. 'But as you've often pointed out yourself, Lafe mixes with smart, moneyed people, and I'm darned if I'll invite Aunt Dora and that loud-mouthed husband of hers. I won't be shown up by him ... too much is at stake for me, possibly my entire future.'

'If Lafe Sheridan wants you, my girl, then he won't hold it against you that your relatives happen to be working class,' her aunt retorted. 'His own beginnings were even more humble than ours!'

'Lafe had the brains and the ambition to get out of the rut.' Gale fingered the lovely brooch which he had recently given her, a topaz that matched her eyes. 'You know as well as I do, Aunt Sue, that Uncle Ben will get at the drink and start one of those class-war arguments of his. Lord and Lady Bazeley have been invited to the party and it would annoy Lafe if there was any unpleasantness. Aunt, sweetie, do be reasonable.'

Eden was playing draughts with Uncle Harry and their eyes met in amusement across the board. Gale would get her own way. She always did.

When Friday evening came, Gale persuaded Eden to spend the week-end at Bellevue with her. She wanted to be on the spot to supervise the final party arrangements, and added laughingly that she didn't dare to shock Aunt Sue by spending the weekend alone with a couple of bachelors.

Gareth drove the sisters to the house, and Gale at once assumed the smiling graciousness of a hostess as she conducted Eden into a delightful bedroom. 'I advised Lafe on fittings for the bedrooms,' she said proudly. 'Lafe is particularly male. He doesn't realize the importance to a woman of sleeping in an attractive bedroom.'

Eden glanced round at the cream-coloured furniture with silver fittings and silvery-green carpeting. The bed held shell-shaped projections curving out from the head of it; one of them held books, the other an elegant reading lamp. The long silk curtains were a pale apricot colour to match the bedspread. The long windows overlooked the downs, and made her think of the evening she and Lafe had sat in his car and talked about 'the tiger he had to keep riding.'

'You have wonderful taste, Gale,' she murmured.

'All I needed was the money to let myself go.' Gale sighed happily. 'Wait till you see my dress! It's a model. A gift from Lafe, of course.'

'Mine's in my case,' Eden said with a grin.

'Then for heaven's sake unpack it before it gets crushed.' Gale made an elegant exit from Eden's room, already in her own mind mistress of Beelevue.

CHAPTER THREE

THE following morning Eden and Gareth went for a stroll on the downs. The lilac mist of lady's smock still lingered, mingling with the dropped butter of cowslips. The wind was tangy with hill and woodland scents, and they scrambled laughingly to a kingly sweep of downland. Here it was like standing on a green velvet cloud and Eden, like a suddenly startled faun, took flight with Gareth in pursuit. They dived with youthful abandon through the green bracken, past clumps of purple harebells, down a slope that tipped her into a patch of sunlit grass.

She lay breathless and laughing, boyish in her tapered trews and cuddle-collar sweater.

Gareth threw himself down beside her and they lay on their backs watching mare's tails in the sky, their fingertips lightly touching. 'This is indeed a precious Eden,' Gareth murmured. Then he lifted himself on an elbow and gazed down at the girl beside him. 'How well your name suits you, Eden. All this peace, all this solitary charm is in you ... Eden.'

He held her a captive in the grass. She could see herself reflected in the pupils of his eyes, and age-old feminine wisdom warned her not to fight him.

'All this fresh air has given me an appetite,' she smiled. 'I shall eat an enormous lunch when we get back to Bellevue.'

His eyes roamed her face, rose-stung by the downland breezes; his gaze lingered on the innocently inviting fullness of her underlip. 'D'you know something?' he whispered.

She shook her head, the thud of his heart against her.

'I've never kissed a girl in the grass.'

Longing ached in his eyes, and Eden lay passive, feeling his warm breath, his hands holding her shoulders, then his kiss made clumsy by his shy eagerness. Why did she submit like this? Was it because Lafe had decreed that she give happiness to this talented ward of his?

'How different you are from other girls,' Gareth murmured against her cheek.'

'Have you known many?' she enquired.

'A few, out in Cape Town, but none of them were as excitingly elusive as you. Eden, what do you feel about me?'

'I like you, Gareth.'

'I want to be more than liked—by you.' He stroked an errant lock of hair from one of her winged eyebrows and searched her wide brown eyes. 'You've never been in love, have you, Eden?'

She shook her head, and felt her heart beat fast. She wanted to jump to her feet, to flee from these intimate questions. Love had become something she didn't want to talk about.

'Does it alarm you, the thought of falling in love?' His smile faintly teased her. 'You can't run free as a faun all your life. You've got to give yourself to a man one day.'

'Gareth, don't get serious,' she pleaded, 'not just yet.'

'I'm just giving you warning of my intentions.' He dropped a kiss on her nose, then leapt to his feet and pulled her up with him. She broke free of him with a laugh and they raced home to Bellevue.

They entered the house to find Gale having words with Donovan, a manservant of Lafe's. He had broken a rather valuable ornament, but with Irish unconcern he was sweeping up the pieces and informing Gale that he had been breaking things belonging to 'himself' for a long time now, but 'himself' was not a man to be putting pots before the flesh.

'You're careless and arrogant, Donovan!' There were angry flushes on Gale's high cheekbones. 'You'll have to learn to be more careful with valuable objects if you expect to remain in *my* employ.'

' 'Tes Mr. Sheridan who employs me, miss. And seems like there are one or two things you'll have to be learning yourself. Himself gives the orders, and a pretty bit of skirt won't be after changing him.'

Gale was left gaping as Donovan stalked away

with the brush and pan, and as he passed Eden he lowered a deliberate wink at her.

'I can't stand that insolent creature!' Gale stormed. 'He not only drinks, but he's totally inefficient. I can't think why Lafe puts up with him!'

Gareth, hands in the pockets of his slacks, was regarding Gale with unsmiling eyes. 'Donovan saved Lafe's life out in Africa some years ago,' he said quietly. 'Lafe was using dynamite to clear some of his land of rock; a blast wasn't timed correctly and he was knocked unconscious. Donovan raced and dragged him clear of the second blast which would have blown him into fragments. Sure, Miss Ellis, Donovan likes his nip of whisky, but I advise you not to complain about him to Lafe.'

Gale's eyes went narrow, almost cat-like. 'I don't take advice from Lafe's hangers-on,' she sharply retorted.

'Gale!'

Eden gave her sister a shocked look. Gareth, with a slight shrug of his shoulders, went striding up the stairs to his music-room.

'That was an unforgivable thing to say to Gareth,' Eden exclaimed.

Gale's eyes swept over Eden, taking in her wind-tossed hair and the wisps of grass that clung to her sweater and her trews. 'You look as though you've been enjoying a romp in the grass with dear Gareth,' she drawled. 'But I mean to put a stop to

43

all this imposing on Lafe's generosity.'

'You do quite a bit of that yourself, Gale, with less excuse than Gareth or Donovan ... who both love him!'

'How dare you say that to me!' Gale's slender figure tautened with anger, her fingernails curled in against the sleekness of her skirt.

'I say it because it happens to be true.' Eden stood blade-trim before Gale, roused to temper by the mercenary streak in her sister. 'You don't know the first thing about loving anyone but yourself. It means nothing to you that you've hurt Tony. You only want Lafe because he's richer ... because he can take you out of Lowton. You've angled for that ever since the night we first met him.'

'Have I now?' Gale's eyes were slits of saffron, fixed upon Eden with a glittering curiosity. 'What's the matter, Eden, are you jealous because he chose to prefer me to a half-baked kid? Have you got a secret crush on him?'

Even as Gale's voice rang out alarmingly in the hall, Eden saw the door of Lafe's study swing open. His tall figure stepped into the hall ... almost certainly he had caught the tail end of Gale's remark.

'I should have thought you'd have guessed before now, Gale, how things stand between *Gareth* and me.' Then quick as a flash she darted up the stairs, hastened into her bedroom and quickly shut the door behind her. She threw herself across the bed,

44

trembling with reaction, unable to stop, confirmed now in the fear that had haunted her from the moment she had looked into Lafe's eyes in the tumbling snow.

She loved him!

The truth blazed in her brain ... in her heart .... she loved the man who wanted her beautiful sister, and a reckless lie was preferable to having him pity her!

Gale had never let a spat with Eden trouble her very much, and their recent one over Gareth was forgotten by her when she came to her young sister's room just before the party.

She wore white chiffon-silk, classically draped about her lovely figure. An orchid from Lafe tumbled on her left shoulder, clinging there like a mauve spider. Her Mona Lisa hairstyle suited her to perfection, blending with the small, self-aware smile at the corners of her pink mouth. Her eyes were brilliant with excitement and hazel-pearl make-up.

'Aren't you dressed yet?' she exclaimed.

Eden, clad in a lacy slip, was putting on her nylons. She still looked rather pale, but she never bore grudges and was warm in her praise of Gale's glamorous appearance. 'I love your orchid, it's so weird and wonderful.'

Gale stood admiring her reflection in the triple mirrors of the dressing-table. 'My black Irishman knows *my* expensive tastes and doesn't mind catering for them, despite what you said to me earlier on, sweetie.' Her glance fell on the plastic box on the toilet table. She lifted the lid and disclosed a single pink rose.

'From Gareth, I bet?' Gale smiled.

Eden was slipping into her dress, wild-rose silk, the skirt ruched, the neckline a youthful scoop that revealed the vulnerable hollows of her throat and shoulders, and the way her hair feathered at the nape of her slim neck.

'Gareth must have slipped the rose into my room while I was soaking in the tub.' Eden felt touched by the gesture and thought it typical of him to make it in such a modest fashion. 'Whereabouts shall I wear my flower, Gale?'

'Here, I think.' Gale took the rose and pinned it near Eden's heart. 'That should flatter the young man, to see that your heart flutters beneath his rose. Sweetie,' Gale's self-assured smile faltered, 'I'm sorry for what I said about Gareth. I was so annoyed with Donovan that I let my tongue run away with me.' Her fingers travelled the slender length of Eden's arms. 'I had no idea you'd fallen for Gareth. You are rather a closed book when it comes to your feelings, kitten.'

Eden turned to the toilet table and patted her nose and cheeks with a powder-puff. 'Gareth's very sensitive, and it isn't true that he's a hanger-on. He's been with Lafe since he was a schoolboy.

they're like brothers ... and Lafe fairly glows with satisfaction when he listens to Gareth at the piano.'

'Enough said!' Gale gave a husky laugh. 'I'll never dare to say another word against your blue-eyed boy.'

'His eyes are sorrel-brown,' Eden corrected.

'You've been gazing into their sorrel depths, I take it?'

Eden couldn't meet her sister's eyes, and was about to clasp a string of pink corals about her throat when they were whisked out of her hands. 'You don't need those!' Gale's fashion-conscious glance took Eden in from her silver slippers to her elfin head. A rather startled gleam came into her eyes.

'You've become quite fetching, my pet,' she drawled. She twined an arm about Eden's and they stood together in front of the long mirrors of the dressing-table, one sister possessed of a striking attraction whose impact was immediate, the other with a woodland appeal that caught the eye and eluded it. 'The orchid and the rose,' Gale laughed.

They curtsied to their reflections, then left the room and made their way down the gracefully curving staircase to the hall. Lafe rose from an oak settle and came towards them, a gladiator in dark evening wear, his black hair and lashes intensifying the vivid green of his Irish eyes. He was smoking a cigar and Eden's nostrils tensed to the strong aroma of it, while her pulses went slightly crazy as his eyes rested a moment on the rose she wore against her heart.

His firm lips curved into a smile. 'You both look enchanting,' he said. 'My house is honoured.'

'You sound like a Regency gallant.' Gale stood close to him for a moment, her fingertips stealing along the breadth of his shoulders, then she swept away to the dining-room to ensure that the long table had been laid as she had ordered. The house smelled of flowers, and the chandeliers sparkled overhead. The furniture and the panelling gleamed with beeswax.

'We've ten minutes before the invasion,' Lafe took Eden by the elbow. 'Come to my snug and have a sherry.'

In a slight panic she glanced up the stairs, on the verge of saying she had forgotten her handkerchief. Lafe quirked an eyebrow at the glance. 'Gareth isn't going to run away,' he drawled. 'Though I understand how you feel, of course. Love is inclined to bring with it a feeling of anxious insecurity, only assuaged when the beloved is within sight and sound.'

He sounded faintly mocking, as if he knew that Gale was never likely to feel like that about him ... even though he might feel like it about her.

Almost unaware, Eden walked with him into his snug, where he opened a cabinet which contained bottled and wine glasses. She glimpsed a vodka label and asked brightly for a vodka and tonic. He

48

swung round to her and quizzed her from head to foot. 'Have you had it before?' he demanded.

'No, but I've a sudden urge to try something potent.' She walked to the fireplace, the hem of her wild-rose dress swaying. A cork popped behind her, liquid was poured liberally, there was a tinkle of ice. A glass decorated with cherries was placed in her hand. 'Try that,' Lafe ordered. She took several sips and found the drink delicious.

'Is this a Sheridan special?' she smiled.

'Yes, and much safer for little girls than vodka.'

'I'm not a little girl,' she protested. 'I shall be twenty in September.'

'A mighty great age,' he mocked, taking a mouthful of his whisky sour. 'I suppose because Gale is a natural sophisticate, you're developing a yen to be like her?'

'Well, I am supposed to look a little like her.' Eden smiled slowly and knew it to be a conscious imitation of Gale's. Lafe wasn't amused. His eyes went cold as green ice.

'Don't start imitating Gale,' he said curtly. 'Grow up in your own way—be an original, not a copy.'

She flushed, stung by the implication that she could never be as provocative or as lovely as Gale. 'I was only kidding,' she said stiffly. 'When you're young, you're uncertain of almost everything except your own goucheries ... impatient to have people treat you like a responsible adult.'

'Vodka's the road to irresponsibility,' he said drily.

She glanced up, faintly returned his smile, the small dimples gliding in and out beneath her cheekbones.

'Take a bit of advice from a man almost double your age, Eden.' His voice was crushed velvet again, with a brooding undertone of Irish music in it. 'Stay young as long as possible, for the responsibilities of adulthood are with us much longer than the rainbows of adolescence.'

'They're rather clouded rainbows at times— Lafe.'

'Ah, but the clouds roll by, Eden, and the sun comes out for the young and innocent as it can never come out for those who have attained sophistication.'

Eden scanned his forceful, hard-bitten face, which the trenchant years of building up a big business had marked with a certain ruthlessness. If in his own youth he had cherished dreams of a different love from the kind Gale would give him, he had long since abandoned those dreams.

Then as a glint of curiosity came into his green eyes, Eden moved away from him to a window. The curtains had not yet been drawn and the evening shadows were cut open by the lights of an approaching car.

'Your guests have begun to arrive,' she said.

With that noiseless walk peculiar to big men

Lafe had come to stand behind her. She tensed, acutely aware of him towering above her. There ran through her a sudden longing for his hard arms around her, holding her close, wanting her as she wanted him.

'Bellevue must have known many parties in the past,' he mused. 'Carriages would have rolled down the driveway, and uniforms would have glittered beside the silk and velvet of lovely gowns.'

'The music of a waltz would have drifted down from the gallery, while the proud mammas sat in a bunch, fluttering their fans and plotting matrimony for their daughters,' Eden smiled.

'Lafe!'

Gale's voice broke in upon them, and Eden drew quickly away from Lafe as her sister sailed into the room. 'The Wintons have just arrived, darling.' She took hold of his arm, possessively. 'Do come and say hullo to them.'

The party turned out to be a glittering success for Gale. She had chosen and mixed the guests as deftly as though she had been doing it for years, and there was no denying the fact that she and Lafe made a striking couple—both self-assured, good at making conversation, gifted with that indefinable quality called personality.

After dinner there was dancing to an orchestra in the ballroom with its chandeliers, long mirrors, and alcoves where flowers were massed.

Gareth's chin came down hard against Eden's soft hair as they drifted to the rhythm of a slow foxtrot. 'Clever of you to wear a rose with your rose-coloured dress,' he murmured.

They executed a turn in the dance, and Eden's heart whirled with it. She had been sure that Gareth had given her the rose, now she remembered Lafe's eyes upon it as she and Gale had come down the stairs. Having given Gale a flower, he had ensured that her young sister had one as well!

She gazed around the ballroom until her eyes found him, the tallest man in the room, laughing with Gale and the Wintons, close friends of his who lived at Hove.

There was a high, wide, buccaneer air about him tonight that rang in his laughter, and some time later Eden found herself dancing in his arms. He was amazingly graceful, his arms at once a heaven and a hell for her. It seemed that all her life she had been waiting for Lafe Sheridan to put his arms around her ... when their dance came to an end she had to brace herself to bear the pain of coming apart from him.

'Thanks, kitten,' he said.

She forced a casual smile to her lips, and dropped him a curtsy.

Towards midnight the fun slowed down and guests began to say their adieus. Cars began to roll away from the house, and fallen petals lay on the floor of the ballroom as Eden and Gareth strolled the length of it, idly talking.

'Your rose is crushed.' He fingered it against her bosom. 'It must have happened while we danced.'

She nodded, but she knew that it was in Lafe's arms that the rose had become crushed. After parting from him, she had put up a hand to touch the rose and had found it broken.

'It was a good party,' said Gareth. 'Everyone was bedazzled by your sister. Everyone thinks she'll make the perfect wife for Lafe.'

They reached the door of the empty ballroom and as they stepped out into the hall, they saw Gale on the front steps with Lafe, waving goodbye to the last of their guests.

The Wintons were persuaded by Lafe to stay overnight, and Sunday turned out to be such a warm, sunny day that the swimming-pool was used for the first time. Gale was in her element, gaily at ease with Lafe's friends, racing with him in the green pool, loafing on a sun mattress.

Eden sat in a rattan chair, flicking the pages of a magazine and watching Lafe unobserved through sun-glasses. He lounged in bronze-coloured trunks near the edge of the pool, his thick dark hair tousled from the water, a long drink in his hand as he yarned with Sammy Winton about hunting trips they had taken together in Africa. Sammy and his wife had farmed out there for a couple of years ... and Eden noticed that Gale was inclined to look bored by these African tales.

All at once her sister stretched a curvaceous leg towards Lafe and drew her foot down one of his long, sinewy legs. It was a gesture that said: 'Remember me? I'm still here.'

He quirked a look at her, and Eden's fingers tightened on her magazine at the ruthless smile on his mouth. He swept Gale's bikini-clad body with his green eyes. 'I haven't forgotten you, you lovely witch,' his look seemed to say. 'I'm well aware of you.'

Gareth stretched himself in a chair beside Eden's. 'Shall we take a run in the car this afternoon?' he suggested.

'Good idea.' Eden met his smile ... eager to get away from Bellevue ... desperately eager.

She carried her overnight bag out to the car when they left after lunch for their drive. She had decided not to return to Bellevue for dinner.

'Had a good time, pixie?' Lafe stood on the steps and looked big and carefree, a green shirt thrown open at his throat, his hands in the pockets of tailored slacks.

'It's been lots of fun,' she assured him. 'Thanks for inviting me.'

'You're always welcome at Bellevue, Eden. This is Gareth's home as much as mine.'

He waved them off, and Eden had to fight with herself not to glance back and catch one more glimpse of his tall figure. The car turned out of the drive and on to the public highway. 'At last we're alone,' said Gareth. 'Are you as pleased as I am?'

She nodded, for how could she hurt him? 'Yes, it's good to be alone at last,' she said, her hands clenched in her lap.

'What's the betting we'll soon be hearing of an engagement?' he shot a look at her, the breeze whipping his hair. 'Will you like Lafe for a brother-in-law?'

Eden's fingernails stabbed her hands. 'Of course I will.'

Liar. The word screamed through her mind. 'You'd like Lafe for yourself ... yourself!'

She hardly knew why this was so, for he frightened her with his hardness even as he melted her with his strange flashes of tenderness. He was years older, steeped in worldliness, and attracted by Gale. Yet Eden was in no doubt about her feelings ... she loved the man who one week later was to give her sister an emerald and diamond engagement ring.

CHAPTER FOUR·

EDEN was in bed asleep when the light flicked on, waking her from a queer dream in which she had been lost in a storm. There had been thunder, lightning, even rain ... there was still a wetness on her cheeks ... teardrops she hastily brushed away when she saw Gale seated on the side of her bed, looking lovely with her dark hair piled on top of her head, her topaz eyes glowing and golden, as they always were when she was thrilled about something.

'Do you like it?' She thrust her left hand almost under Eden's nose.

'W-what?' Eden was still sleep confused.

'My ring, sweetie!' Gale moved her hand back and forth so the stones flashed. 'It's big enough for you to see, surely? Lafe gave it to me tonight.'

Eden pushed herself into a sitting position and gazed at the ring. Oh, yes, it was certainly big enough. A glowing, chunky emerald with a surround of fiery diamonds, green and white fire against the smooth white skin of Gale's hand.

'I've got him!' Gale exulted. 'Congratulate me, kitten.'

Eden had known all along that this moment must come, but words of congratulation were locked in her throat, and her sister grew irritated by her lack of excited response to the lustrous ring that proclaimed her the intended wife of Lafe Sheridan ... self-made tycoon, ruthless-faced Irishman, whom many women had angled for and failed to land. Gale *had* landed him and she was suitably triumphant.

With half-laughing exasperation she caught at Eden's slight shoulders and gave her a shake. 'Wake up, say something, even if it's only "lord help you!" I believe it's what you're thinking!'

'N-no——'

'Then why are you looking so—shocked?' Though Gale laughed, her topaz eyes had suddenly narrowed.

Eden saw this and made an effort to pull herself together. 'Of course I'm pleased for you, Gale— congratulations.'

'Said like an obedient little girl,' Gale mocked. 'You're getting as bad as Aunt Sue. She seems to regard Lafe as a sort of iron man with thunder and fire beneath his skin instead of flesh and blood. I know, let's see how you look in my fabulous ring!'

This suggestion sent Eden shying back against her pillows. 'No—please——'

'Don't be such a prim little puss.' Gale forcibly captured Eden's left hand and slid the ring on to the third finger. Then she held the small, cold hand and laughed with real amusement. 'How odd it looks on you, baby!'

It looked heavy, almost brash on Eden's thin young hand with its filed, unpainted fingernails, and she was glad to remove its expensive weight from her hand. Gale returned it to her own third finger, her mouth lush with triumph rather than tremulous with love. There was little love for Lafe, the man, in Gale's heart, and with sudden sharp agony Eden said to her:

'Have you seen Tony lately?'

If Gale was startled or angered by the question it didn't show on her face. 'No, I haven't seen many of my old friends just lately,' she rejoined coolly.

'I—I saw him last night.' Eden plucked at the sheet nervously. 'I thought he was looking—rather run-down.'

Gale slowly lifted her gaze from her ring, a slight frown drew her delicate eyebrows together.

'Gareth and I went to see *Is Your Honeymoon Really Necessary?* Tony was in the foyer of the theatre and we had a few words with him.' Eden gazed at Gale and gathered her breath. 'Be sure that you're doing the right thing, Gale. Don't marry Lafe if—if you really love Tony.'

'Are you asking me if my honeymoon is really necessary?' A sudden flash of temper glittered in Gale's eyes. 'If you are, then you've got a darned cheek!'

'Gale,' Eden threw out an appealing hand, almost as if to ward off an expected blow, 'I know you, and I know how you feel about Tony in your heart of hearts.

'What schoolgirl nonsense,' Gale scoffed. 'I care for Tony as a friend. Lafe is decidedly the man I'm going to marry.'

'You're selling and he's buying,' Eden said bitterly.

Gale caught her breath, not at the crude truth of the remark, but because it was the first time she had ever heard Eden say anything like it. From Eden, because she was charitable, the remark both shocked and stung.

'What would you know about it?' Gale demanded. 'The only real boy-friend you've ever had is Gareth Conway, and now you're talking as though you know it all. Has Gareth been initiating you into the secrets of the love game?'

Eden winced at the rather cruel edge to Gale's voice. Gale stood up and went to the dressing-table, where she stood removing the topaz eardrops which were also a gift from Lafe. 'What did Tony have to say?' she asked carelessly. 'Did he mention me?'

'He asked how you were.'

'And you told him I was blooming?'

'I said you were keeping well.'

'And that I was keeping with Lafe?'

'We—didn't mention Lafe.'

'Why ever not? Lafe's been the biggest topic of conversation in Lowton for the past eight weeks. Don't tell me the three of you weren't bursting to mention him—or should I say four? Was Tony escorting a girl?'

'No, he was on his own.'

'Tony's a sentimental mug—yes, he is, Eden! He thought we could live on love in a cottage. Me in a frilly apron, cooking the eggs and keeping an eye on the baby in our box of a garden. Lord, I'd stifle to death! I want big rooms and fabulous furniture —to the devil with love on a pittance!'

Gale flashed a glittering smile at Eden. 'Stop looking so pained, sugar-pie. Lafe knows exactly what he's *buying* ... you should have heard the way he laughed at all the arrant nonsense in the *Lowton Gazette* about our fairy-tale romance. Lafe has never mistaken me for Cinderella. He's no such fool.'

'When do you plan to marry?' Eden's lips moved stiffly. 'Have you set a date?'

'We both fancy the end of July, and you are going to be one of my bridesmiads.'

Eden's hands clenched her bedcovers, her mouth was suddenly as blanched as her fine-boned face. 'Do I have to be one?' she appealed. 'You know how I dislike dressing up.'

Gale stared at her young sister, her hands suspended in the act of unzipping her dress. 'Tonight you're quite the little girl who wouldn't say yes! Of course you're going to be my chief bridesmaid, and I've already decided to put you in lemon chiffon. You'll look rather distant and touching.' Gale smiled as she peeled off her dress and stood

60

slim and seductive in wisps of nylon lingerie. 'When Gareth sees you he'll demand your shy hand in marriage.'

'Gareth and I are just good friends....'

'Come off it, sweetie. You're no actress, and it's obvious you like the lad. You're unlikely to find another prospect like him in this dull hole of a town.' Gale admired her emerald embedded in diamonds. 'Just think of it, Eden, the two Ellis girls, the Orphan Annies of Lowton, in the money and thumbing their noses at the world. I *shall*, and you could. Gareth has talent, and later on he'll make a packet of money with his music.'

Gale began to brush her dark hair, her engagement ring flashing with barbaric splendour. 'I want to honeymoon somewhere exotic and wildly expensive, where all the best people go.'

'Gale——'

'Yes, sweetie?' Gale turned from the mirror, and then cooed indulgently: 'Will it put your funny little mind at rest if I admit that I find my future bridegroom a very attractive person? Women look at him when we go places—and I really find that exciting.'

Eden sank back against her pillows, her heart in a vice. Lafe was the boss of Sheridan's, the brain, the power, the imagination behind it all, but Gale had not discovered that there was still a boy in him at times. A lonely boy, who needed to be loved for himself, not just for his money and his physical attractiveness.

'Eden,' Gale's eyes held the complacent gleam of a cream-fed cat's, 'I believe I've done something my king of commerce wasn't quite counting on ... can you guess what it is?'

Eden wanted to die ... to curl up and die rather than face that look in Gale's eyes.

'He's fallen for me, Eden. I saw it in his eyes to-night, just after he gave me this.' Gale caressed the lustrous ring. 'You can imagine how excited I was at getting it, and he said I looked no more than a kid, with flushed cheeks and stars in my eyes ... and that was when he gave himself away. He looked at me as though—as though he couldn't believe I was real ...

'Eden, I've never seen Lafe look like that before ... I could tell he was bowled over to think he'd proposed and I'd accepted him.'

On the Saturday morning following Gale's engagement to Lafe, Eden decided to call on old Rosie Barrat before taking a bus into Redford where she intended to buy her sister an engagement present.

Rosie was one of the old folks whose cottage was due to be pulled down, and Eden knew how upset she was at the prospect. Since the death of her soldier son in Aden she was all alone in the world, a chirpy little woman who had done office cleaning before her plaguey rheumatics had got the better of

62

her. One of her regular places had been the insurance office which Eden's uncle managed.

Old Sam Carstairs was repairing the trellis over his porch, and Eden paused to have a few words with him. They talked about his budding roses, one of which found its way into Eden's lapel. 'Me and Sarah ain't blaming you, Miss Eden, for what them council people are going to do to us,' he said.

'I know, Sam.' Eden slipped the money for some tobacco into the pocket of his baggy cardigan. 'I'm on my way to see Mrs Barrat. The poor dear is worried about her cat. I've offered to have him, but Rosie seems to think he'll fret or run away if he's separated from her.'

'Aye, old Rosie sets great store by that ginger cat her Alfie gave her. Seems a pity he'll have to go when they turn us out of our homes ... I've heard it said, Miss Eden, that the council could have bought other land for a bit more money and left our cottages alone. Is it a fact?'

She nodded. 'They just won't meet the price that's being asked for the site, Sam. These cottages are council owned, and as they're rather old they're reckoned redundant.'

'Like us folks who live in them,' he said morosely. 'We're old and they-want to shut us up in boxes, one way or t'other.'

'Cheer up, Sam.' Eden squeezed his arm. 'Something might turn up yet.'

'Aye,' he smiled and touched his rosebuds. 'When you look at roses, you know there can be miracles.'

His words kept running through Eden's mind as she made her way further along the lane to Rosie's cottage. Poignant the scent of roses and the memory they evoked of a hothouse bloom crushed in the arms that belonged around the slender figure of her sister.

Eden loved Rosie's kitchen, with its tea kettle singing on the hob, its white-painted farmhouse chairs, and berry-sprigged curtains at the tiny windows. Marmie was curled up on the sill among the flower pots, blinking a green eye in the sunlight.

'The *Lowton Gazette* is full of your sister's engagement.' Rosie was bustling about making a pot of tea and laying out a plate of jam puffs. 'How has your Aunt Sue taken the news? I know she's none too set on that stir-about Irishman.'

'My aunt always hoped she'd marry Dr. Gregg's son, but she'll get used to the idea of having Lafe Sheridan as a nephew-in-law.' Eden met Rosie's searching glance and smiled brightly. 'He's given Gale a rajah of a ring, a great chunky emerald surrounded by diamonds.'

'Sounds just the sort of ring she'd like.' Rosie spoke tartly. 'Has she fixed a date for the wedding?'

'The end of July.'

'Pleased yourself about the engagement?' Rosie handed her a cup of tea. Some of it spilled into the saucer as Eden took it, and Rosie was quick to notice the tremor of her hand. 'Glory be, girl, don't tell me you've taken a shine to the man yourself?'

'I—I like him, of course——'

'I've known you a long time, my dearie, and I know when you're upset about something. What is it?' Rosie looked shrewd. 'You like him and think he's being married for his money?'

'He cares for Gale——'

'And that one cares more for herself. Aye, I know, Eden. I've been on this earth too long not to be able to figure folks.' Rosie sat at the kitchen table and sipped her tea. 'He's a well-favoured chap, eh? Some Irishman are, especially about the eyes.'

'He's tremendously energetic,' Eden smiled, 'with a rather imperative manner, as though he thinks of life as a big operation and himself as chief surgeon.'

'Sounds a bit bossy, and I can't imagine your sister being bossed about by a man. She's the type to want to wear the pants.'

Eden had to laugh. Lafe, she assured Rosie, was the last man on earth to surrender his pants to a woman.

'I must say you look a bit more heartsome now you've had a laugh.' Rosie broke an oat-cake and spread it with cottage cheese. 'Want a piece of this, lass?'

'I'm going to try a jam puff.' Eden sank her teeth into a feathery puff bursting with home-made jam. 'Mmmm, delicious.'

'My old fireside oven bakes a tasty batch of cakes and pies, and I don't know how I'll manage without it.' Rosie sighed and Eden watched as her eyes dwelt on each well-loved nook of her warm, scrubbed kitchen. On the old wooden dresser, bright with china and a few pieces of burnished pewter. On the fender stool where Marmie slept of a night ... on the mantelpiece where there were photographs of her son.

'It does no good to fret myself, but I always reckoned on spending my last days here in the cottage where I came as a bride ... and talking about brides, I suppose you'll be one of Gale's bridesmaids?'

Eden nodded. 'She's having six. I'm on my way into Redford to buy her an engagement present.'

An hour later Eden was making her way across Redford's main road to the glassware shop where she hoped to find something to suit her sister. Gale wasn't an easy person to please when it came to gifts, she lacked Eden's appreciation of the eye-catching oddity and preferred something smart ... and expensive.

Eden gazed thoughtfully at lampshades, vases and toilet-table sets, but her glance would keep stealing to a kingfisher fashioned of clear blue glass, its beak plunged in its wing feathers. Would Gale like that, or would she prefer that toilet set in amber glass with silver lids?

Then she nearly jumped out of her skin as a voice like deep, crushy velvet spoke above her head: 'Can't you make up your mind which toy to buy yourself?' the voice enquired.

Eden whirled from the shop window, her heart in her throat as she met the eyes of her sister's fiancé. 'Hullo, Lafe! I'm trying to decide on a present for Gale—an engagement present. I'm terribly pleased for you and Gale—congratulations.'

'Thanks, Eden.' That deep furrow slashed his cheek, and he gestured at the kerb where his car stood. 'I'll collect a ticket if we hang around. Dash into the shop and buy your present, then I'll take you to lunch.'

'Oh—all right.' She hovered, torn between the kingfisher and the toilet set.

'You've got your eye on the bird, eh?'

She felt Lafe's hand against her waist, felt the brush of his lovat-green suit. Her heart was hammering with the painful joy of having him beside her, towering and dark, frightening and beloved.

'It's pretty, but I'm not sure it's Gale's sort of thing. Do you think she'd prefer that toilet set in amber and silver, Lafe?'

'Decidedly. But because I'd hate to see anyone but you in possession of that delectable blue bird, I'm going to buy it for you.'

'I can't let you do that,' she protested.

'What, give my prospective kid sister a toy?' he mocked. He marched her into the shop and ordered the salesgirl to get the bird out of the window. It glowed blue and realistic on the counter, and Eden had to give in and let Lafe give it to her.

A few minutes later they emerged from the shop and Lafe put Eden and her packages into his car. He took the seat beside her and the slam of the door shut them in together. He started up the car and a while later was heading out of Redford into the country. 'I see enough of smart restaurants,' he remarked. 'I suggest we lunch at a rather nice villag pub I know of. Would you like that?'

She nodded. 'I like black-beamed village pubs and the warm burr of country voices,' she smiled.

'How different you are from Gale.' He shot her a look from sooty-lashed eyes. 'Not so much in looks but in ways. You like the simple things, but she likes everything to be smart and up-to-date.'

'You mean I'm unworldly,' Eden murmured. 'Gale would never drool over a glass bird.'

'Hardly.' He chuckled to himself, drily. 'What do you think of her ring? I had it specially made for her.'

'It's a dazzler.' Eden studied his profile and knew by that saturnine slash in his cheek that he wasn't in any way fooled by Gale despite the fact that she had got under his hardened skin with her seductive loveliness. He seemed, in fact, to get as much amusement out of giving Gale an emerald and diamond ring as he had got out of giving Eden the glass kingfisher.

In a while the car came in sight of a village church and then they were passing through the village itself, old-world, with timber-framed houses and shops, a market hall with a bell-tower, and a whipping-post adjacent to the police-station.

Lafe turned the car into the courtyard of a Tudor-fronted inn and halted before a welcoming line of mullioned windows. A massive walnut-tree stood in the centre of the courtyard.

'Hungry?' Lafe asked as he gave her a hand out of the car.

'As a cuckoo-chick.' She guessed the country air had whipped up her appetite, and gazed round with interest as they entered the oak-beamed dining-room of the inn. They sat at a table in a mullioned bay, where Lafe ordered a sherry for Eden and a tankard of ale for himself. They browsed over the menu, Eden very conscious of the brush of Lafe's shoulder and the spicy tang of the after-shave lotion which he used. She broke into a smile when he looked at her over the rim of his tankard.

His green glance encompassed her; it was like going down under the sea, and she turned her head quickly to the window beside them. 'That old tree must have been here in the coaching days,' she said.

'Look at its mass of branches. Wonderful for climbing.'

'Did you used to climb trees when you were a schoolgirl?'

'Yes.' She gave a nostalgic laugh. 'Tony Gregg had a dog called Lolly and once she chased a cat up into a tree in our garden. I went up to get the cat down and was silly enough to lose my footing. *That* cured me of climbing trees.'

'You mean you fell out of the tree?'

'Mm. I hurt my back a little.'

'Remember the evening you fell in front of my car?'

'How it snowed, and how fast you were driving! You terrified me.'

He quirked an eyebrow. 'Do I still terrify you, Eden? Do you wish I wasn't going to be your brother-in-law?'

Her heart missed a beat. 'W-what do you mean, Lafe?'

'Wouldn't you prefer Tony Gregg, for instance? Now don't look all wide-eyed. I have big ears and I heard weeks ago that young Gregg was Gale's boyfriend and not yours. I heard he was in the running for the prize, until I pipped him at the post.'

'Lafe, you are cynical,' she protested. 'Why do you always make out you're hard and without any gentle feelings?'

'Hush, little one, it's a secret that I can get sentimental.' He laughed and drained his tankard.

70

'I guess it's come as quite a shock to a number of people that I've succumbed to the lure of matrimony, but most of us are driven to it in the end ... perhaps out of loneliness as much as desire. A man knows what to do about desire ... loneliness is something else.'

The waiter came with their food and over the meal they talked about other things. They didn't touch on personal matters again and Eden was glad in a way. She loved Lafe too much to be able to bear revelations of loneliness from him and when they left the inn and entered the car she curled herself small and remote from him.

During the drive home to Lowton she found herself mentioning Gareth every now and again. He had become important to her in a new way; she could stand between herself and her feelings for Lafe, make of him a shield for her troubled heart.

'I'm glad you two have hit it off.' Lafe spoke seriously. 'He's a boy with a lot of talent, but I don't want him to shut himself away with his music all the time. I want him to have some fun while he's young. To enjoy the company of the right sort of girl. When I was his age there was no time for fun, no time for falling light-heartedly in love ... I look back and feel a trifle robbed.'

His arm brushed hers as they turned into the road that ran through the heath into Lowton. Eden saw nothing, she only felt, and the realization came to her that in future she must avoid being alone like this with Lafe. Everything he said, every quirk of a black eyebrow, every glance, had more meaning than they were meant to have. Only a denial of this kind of intimacy would tame and subdue her love for him, until it became sisterly and sedate.

'You're proud of all the things you've achieved, though, Lafe?' she said. 'You have the power to help people. That's important.'

'What's the matter, Eden?' he quizzed her. 'You work at the Welfare Centre and it must be trying at times to deal with people you can't really help. Do you let it make you unhappy?'

'You're so shrewd, Lafe.' She drew back in her seat, feeling the quick beating of her heart, suddenly afraid of his keen, penetrating eyes. 'As a matter of fact——'

'Tell me,' he ordered.

So she told him about the cluster of Tudor cottages that were due to be pulled down, and how upset the tenants were at the thought of being moved out of homes they had lived in all or most of their lives. Sam with his roses. Rosie and her cat. Deep-set roots that would bleed when they were torn out. 'There's another site available for the new housing estate, but the council are penny-pinching,' she added fiercely. 'And those old people will pay the price!'

'You take other people's problems very much to heart, don't you, Eden?' Lafe brought the car to a halt in front of the Ellis house. He leaned an arm on the wheel and studied her. 'You can't take everyone's troubles on to your young shoulders and I won't have you trying it on.'

'You won't?' She forced a laugh. 'I don't work for you, Mr. Sheridan. You can't give me orders.'

'Soon you'll be my young sister,' he warned.

'Warning me that you'll make a bossy brother?'

He nodded, reached over and opened the door beside her. For a moment he was very close to her and she felt an alarming turbulence of her pulses, a weak and frightened urge to touch him, and be touched by him.

'Don't forget your packages.' His breath fanned her cheek, and in a panic she leaned over and grabbed the packages and scrambled out of the car. He squirked a smile up at her, his brows very black, his eyes a quizzical green, his mouth a little twisted at the corner.

'Th-thanks for the kingfisher and the lovely lunch, Lafe.'

'You're welcome, brown eyes.' He shut the door of the car and took the wheel, added that he would be calling for Gale later in the evening, and drove off. Eden watched the car turn out of the avenue, and as it did so a cloud covered the sun and the day turned grey. Eden gave a shiver and turned to go indoors.

CHAPTER FIVE

MOST of Gale's trousseau shopping was done in London, but there was one small fly in her jam which really irritated her ... Eden's refusal to go with her on her lavish shopping sprees.

'Why won't you come?' she demanded. 'Shopping's real fun when you've got an unlimited expense account to draw on.'

'I've got my job to study,' Eden replied.

'You could give up work right now, like I have,' Gale drawled. 'Lafe isn't the sort to see my young sister working so hard when he's loaded with cash.'

'I should hope I'm a bit more independent than that!' Eden was disgusted by Gale's readiness to take all she could from her indulgent husband to be.

'I begin to think you're a bit narrow in your outlook, my pet,' Gale rejoined. 'Lafe enjoys being generous, so why shouldn't I encourage his enjoyment? If you'd put away your halo and come shopping with me, it would be even more fun. Eden, you used to like to go with me whenever I bought anything new.'

'That was ages ago——'

'Before I met Lafe, eh?' Gale's lips grew thin. 'Sometimes I wonder if you're jealous—ah, that touched a nerve, didn't it? You're jealous because soon I'll belong exclusively to someone else.'

Eden didn't reply. It was a relief that Gale should assume that she resented Lafe. The truth was that she couldn't bear the thought of being with them when they met in London for lunch or tea. 'Tea at the Ritz,' Gale said dreamily. 'Eden, you don't know what you're missing.'

'Marriage made for material benefits will bring heartache for both of you,' said Aunt Sue. 'You mark my words.'

'Very luxurious heartache,' Gale scoffed.

Gareth didn't talk much about Lafe's approaching marriage, and Eden had a feeling that he had agreed to be best man with much the same misgivings as she had agreed to be chief bridesmaid.

The dresses were being made at a salon in London. The place was a hive of activity, noisy with French chatter, and strewn with gorgeous materials.

The woman in charge of the fitting room, Madame Germaine, talked all the time with pins in her mouth, and Eden, stripped to her slip and swathed in lemon chiffon, was fearfully certain that at any moment some of the pins would slip down the Frenchwoman's throat.

'You are so like your sister, *petite*,' Madame enthused. 'You are almost her measurements, except for the bosom.'

'Am I?' Eden murmured, feeling like a doll as

she was turned this way, then that, while yards of lovely chiffon were pinned into place about her figure. Her feelings resembled a doll's. She felt numb as she listened to all the talk about this exciting, fabulous, Cinderella wedding. Let them all pretend to one another that this was the love match of the year. She could not join in their game ... she had neither the heart for it, nor the mercenary streak that made it possible for people to reap a vicarious pleasure out of the fact that a shop-girl had snaffled a tycoon.

Madame smiled—despite the pins in her mouth —and turned to speak to Gale, who was perched gracefully upon a stool, watching the proceedings with a golden-eyed satisfaction. 'Mees Ellis, how attractive your leetle sister is going to look—do you not think?'

Gale's glance moved over Eden. In her Lowton-bought dresses Eden was neat but not striking, but the cloudy, expensive chiffon released new facets of her personality and blended with the pale softness of her skin in almost a seductive way.

Gale's eyebrows lifted, half startled, half amused. 'All of a sudden you seem grown up,' she mused.

After the fittings were over, Gale and her brides-maids were met by Gareth and taken to a smart teashop quite near the block of offices in which Lafe had his London headquarters. There the girls were provided with cakes and ices and cups of creamy coffee.

Halfway through tea, a tall figure suddenly appeared in the doorway of the shop. Eden sat facing the door and she stiffened in her chair as Lafe came to their table with long, imperative strides. A bronzed hand clapped Gareth on the shoulder. 'Put me among the girls!' Lafe laughed deeply.

Gareth cocked a grin up at his guardian, who then moved round the table to give Gale a kiss on the cheek. She received the tribute with a queenly coolness and watched him make room for another chair between Eden and Debbie Wright.

Debbie broke into a giggle at the amusing sight of a coffee whisper in his large hand.

'Well, harem, did everything go all right at the house of silks?' he enquired, looking rather like a pasha as he surveyed the group of attractive females.

'We had a gorgeous time,' Debbie informed him. 'I'm wearing pale cyclamen, but Eden is wearing lemon. She looks super in lemon.'

'She does, eh?' His smiling green eyes dwelt for a moment on Eden's pensive face, then to her relief he turned his attention to his sister. Oh, God, she thought, burying her nose in her coffee cup, why did Gale want all this fuss? Bridesmaids, a lace and satin gown of white, a bouquet of red roses?

Red roses were for love, glowing, passionate, selfless! They weren't meant to be carried by a bride who was selling herself for a life of easy living.

'You're looking rather glum, Eden,' Lafe remarked abruptly. 'Don't you want to be a bridesmaid?'

He spoke half jestingly, but as she met his keen eyes she knew she had been right to avoid him as much as possible. Her love for him had progressed, it had not stood still as she had hoped. To be in his company, even among others, had become torture. She wanted right now to jump up and run away, but she had to force herself to stay where she was, to smile and tell a lie.

'I wouldn't be human if I wasn't looking forward to wearing a fabulous lemon dress,' she rejoined.

'When you girls have had your fill of cakes, we've a date at Cartier's.' Lafe glanced around the table. 'I thought you young ladies would like pendants for your traditional tokens.'

Murmurs of delight greeted this announcement, while Gale said to her fiancé: 'How generous of you, Lafe—and how clever of you to know exactly what young girls like.'

That saturnine cleft sprang into his cheek. 'Even as she strokes me, she cuts me,' he mocked.

'I was paying you a compliment, darling.' As Gale's hand touched his bronze one on the table, the diamonds of her ring flashed around the exotic lustre of the massive emerald. Lafe turned his hand and captured hers, and there was open mockery in the Irish eyes that caught and held hers.

'The Emerald Isle under seige by the brilliant British,' he drawled. 'Rather an appropriate token for you, my lovely witch.'

Eden watched this by-play behind the shelter of her lashes, and she saw Gale snatch her hand from Lafe's. 'Let's make a move,' she said rather sharply.

The bevy of girls were quickly on their feet, and Debbie caught excitedly at Eden's arm as they made their way out of the teashop. 'Isn't it super of Mr. Sheridan to buy pendants for us?' she whispered. 'Don't you just love him, Eden?'

'Yes,' Eden wanted to cry out. To say it aloud, to shock everyone and not care. 'I love Lafe Sheridan, and I wouldn't care if he picked peat for a living and lived in an Irish shanty.'

Instead, of course, she smiled at Debbie and said he was very kind.

Gareth came to the other side of her. 'Four of us are going on to Cartier's in a cab,' he said. 'The rest of the gang are going to pile into Lafe's car.'

'I love riding in taxi-cabs,' Debbie bubbled, cuddling Eden's arm as Gareth signalled a cab to the kerb. They piled inside, the chatter of the other girls hiding to some extent the fact that Eden was rather quiet.

The pendants which Lafe had ordered for Gale's bridesmaids were hearts fashioned from each girl's birthday stone, set in gold and strung on fine chains.

'I'm thrilled with my lovely pendant and I'll

79

wear it even in bed,' Debbie informed the giver, her young eyes dazzled by the rainbow-opal which declared her among the October born. 'I'm sure it will bring me lots of luck, Mr. Sheridan.'

'I want it to bring you luck, child,' he smiled, and looked rather touched.

'Let me have a look at your pendant, Eden.' Gareth took the glowing sapphire into his hand and admired it. 'The September stone of constancy, eh?'

Gale arched an eyebrow, elegant in a suit the plummy purple of a rich grape. 'You can rest assured, Gareth,' she drawled, 'that Eden will always be constant.'

A match struck sharply and Eden glanced quickly at Lafe. He was lighting a cigarette, and above the flame his eyes were fixed upon Gale. They were dangerously green, almost blazing, then he puffed a cloud of smoke and the blaze was dimmed.

Eden slowly breathed again and thought of what her aunt had said at the beginning of Gale's courtship—that Lafe would marry her and make her his in the fullest sense of the word. He would expect loyalty, and he would want an heir. Gale would be made to give him both ... that look in his eyes had just said so.

In the next week or so Gareth began to practise

hard for his first piano recital, due to take place at a Brighton concert hall only a few days before Gale and Lafe were to be married.

Eden saw rather less of him at this time and was glad of the breathing space. He had begun to hint at an engagement of their own, and there was no denying the fact that she had grown very fond of him. His sensitivity and thoughtfulness were rare qualities these days, and when he spoke of needing her, she felt this to be true. She was also aware of a need of her own ... a need to drown her love for Lafe in Gareth's kisses.

Often she felt amazed at the great depth of change within herself and knew that it had stripped away her teenage look. She knew herself awakened and a woman, and she wanted fulfilment as a woman. She didn't want the years ahead made empty by a hopeless longing for a man she couldn't have.

She could have Gareth ... but she needed time in which to adjust to the idea of marrying him.

Clear thinking was made impossible at home just at present, for the house had become a hive of pre-wedding activity. Friends of Gale's were continually popping in and out, while Aunt Sue was in a perpetual fever of polishing and worrying. Gale was being married at the picturesque Norman church in Lowton, and though the reception was being held at a hotel in the town, her Rolls-Royce wedding cars would leave from her aunt's house.

On Saturday morning Eden felt she just had to get away from the bustle for a few hours alone.

The day was warm, even a trifle humid, and the thought of a walk on the downs was very enticing. Her bus jogged out of Lowton, heading for the gorse-clad, rolling hills that had a way of calling the solitary and the troubled to them, where solace was to be found among their wild flowers, singing birds and wandering flocks of sheep and stubby-tailed lambs.

Eden took a winding gypsy track into the hills, a froth of clematis bushes on her left, and there beyond them the snap of broom pods bursting in the warm sunshine. She plunged into the broom and assisted her climb by clutching at the long, tough grass, soon so high in the hills that she could hear the singing of the wind.

She found herself a couch of fern, where she unwrapped her sandwiches and ate them. After her lunch she sat with knees updrawn, arms wrapped round them, alone but for the far-off bleat of sheep and the graceful swooping birds in a sky almost cobalt in patches.

At last she was alone with her thoughts, free to ponder the events of the past weeks, while insects went about their uncomplicated lives in the grass, and butterflies flirted among the hearthbells. Her gaze wandered over the solitary green slopes all around ... if she agreed to become engaged to Gareth she knew her aunt and uncle would be more than pleased. They liked Gareth. Only the other evening her uncle had admitted to her that Gareth was the kind of young man he had always hoped she would meet.

Eden rested her chin on the hillock of her knees and wondered bleakly why she loved Lafe when there was so much about Gareth that appealed to her. His looks, his chivalry, his ability to charm magic out of a piano keyboard. She wanted to love him, but always there was Lafe ... Lafe.

With a soft, wounded moan she sank full length in the fern, her face on her arms. She closed her eyes and wished she might stay up here and not have to return to the world below, where life had grown so complicated.

She was half asleep, her tousled brown head on her arms, her slim body half lost in the lacy fern, when a shadow fell across her body. A long shadow that didn't move until she moved, turning with the swift alarmed grace of a wild creature.

'Hullo, nymph!'

Her senses were reeling. Lafe ... up here?

Then she pulled herself together and gave him a smile. 'Hullo ... man mountain!'

For standing above her he seemed to tower into the cobalt sky that was now shot with puffs of saffron ... a hot, stormy-looking sky. A green sweater with a plit polo-collar hugged Lafe's broad chest and shoulders, a grin cut one corner of his mobile Irish mouth.

'You sleep like a very young child. Sorry to come trampling into your nursery.'

'I wasn't asleep, just drowsing. What a surprise to see you, Lafe. I should have thought you'd be enjoying a dip in your pool on a sticky afternoon like this.'

'I often come up here for a tramp.' He lowered his long body to the grass beside her. 'It loosens me up after being encased behind a desk all the week. Cigarette?' He held out his case, with Turkish cigarettes on one side and a milder, cork-tipped brand on the other. Eden took a tipped cigarette, and his eyes, twin jades in his dark face, were close to her as he held a flame for her.

'Tell me about Africa.' She spoke on impulse, leaning back on an elbow away from him. 'Is it a very beautiful continent?'

'Beautiful?' Turkish smoke drifted back over his shoulder. 'I've seen beauty in its strange, magical twilights, but it's too large, too rugged, too savage at times to be called beautiful. It's a man's continent, where women are much more pampered than over here in England.'

'Have you told Gale you'll be going back there?'

'Do you think she'll object?' There was a note of sardonic amusement in his voice.

'I've an idea she thinks Africa a bit God-forsaken.'

'When she gets there she'll soon change her mind. The Cape Town shops are every bit as large and glittering as she likes them. Our social life is every bit as scintillating as in London or Paris, and though I live fairly deep in the country, I have a small private place which makes travelling hardly a problem at all. Gale will be the Missus of the Big Boss. She'll get quite a kick out of the fuss that will be made of her.'

Eden looked at him, and was shocked as she caught his hard, almost reckless expression. So might a gambler look!

She lifted her cigarette, took smoke deep into her lungs. He knew that he was gambling on Gale's love, and Eden wondered how her sister could be so blind. Couldn't she see that she was marrying a man who might love like a god? A deeply lonely man, deprived of real affection for most of his life and ready to adore his bride?

The intensity of her thoughts made Eden's eyes burn like cornelians, her slight bosom tautened under the check material of her shirt, her heart hammered as Lafe ran his glance over her. A searching glance that narrowed his green eyes.

'How strange,' he murmured, 'right this moment you don't look a bit like Gale.'

'I'm not beautiful like Gale. It's only now and then that we seem alike.'

'You're fey, Eden. Poised for flight at any moment.' He took a hard pull at his cigarette. 'How's the blue kingfisher? Not broken yet?'

'No, I take care of my possessions.'

'And still cling to your nursery treasures, eh? The woolly lamb you used to cuddle in bed? The doll with all the paint washed off her cheeks?' His mockery was light and teasing.

Colour flamed in Eden's cheeks. Gale had been letting him into a few secrets, and the thought of them sharing laughter at her expense was mortifying.

'Gale breaks her things,' she rejoined. 'She always did ... she never cared for anything long enough to treasure it.'

'I can imagine.' A brooding look came into his eyes. 'What we are as children we are as adults ... like tigers we can't change our stripes.'

'Lafe,' Eden touched his sleeve, and then asked breathlessly how Gareth was getting along at his music. She had to remember all the time not to let her feelings for Lafe get the upper hand. Touching him was prohibited, and she took her hand away and plucked a daisy.

They discussed Gareth's coming recital. Did she know that *Woodland Nymph* was included in his programme? She nodded, and didn't miss the smile that came and went at the corner of Lafe's mouth. Then his glance swung to the sky, where a group of ominous-looking clouds were swimming by like enormous fish in a smoky bowl. Birds fell through the sky like dark leaves and a sultry wind carried a faint rumbling sound from the direction of the sea.

'Sure as I am that roast chickens don't lay eggs, there's going to be a storm.' Lafe leapt to his feet. 'Come, Eden, we'd better be moving.'

Eden took the hand he offered and felt his fingers close hard and warm on hers as he pulled her to her feet. 'W-we go in opposite directions.' She brushed grass from her trews and didn't look at him, for parting from him always hurt so much. 'I'm catching a bus back to Lowton.'

'No, you'd better come with me.' His hand closed again around her slender left wrist. 'Those buses are always a devil of a time coming along, and you'll get soaked if this storm should suddenly break. Have tea at the house with Gareth and me, then I'll drive you home. I have a date with Gale, so you'll not be putting me out.'

It would be useless to protest, for already he was striding the opposite way, towards Bellevue, taking her with him. A strange, uncanny silence lay over the downs, then thunder growled, while a steel flicker of lightning lit the sky.

Eden caught her breath, both at the lightning and at the arm which Lafe slung about her waist. The next second he was racing her through the sudden deluge towards an old white windmill whose sails spun above them as they swooped in through the doorway. The place was dim and deserted, echoing to their breathless laughter as they stood wiping rain from their faces. Overhead the lightning and thunder imitated the flash and roar of artillery.

'Lucky for us this place was handy ... faith, I'd forgotten it could storm like this in England.'

They watched the lightning, stabbing down out of the sky like the prongs of a giant rake.

Eden felt Lafe close to her shoulder, his eyes glinting in the dimness of their shelter, a dynamo himself of simmering vitality. A man who enjoyed danger. A man with whom you could share it and not be afraid. Too near, too dear, with a warm, muscular arm twining suddenly about her waist, shooting an intolerable thrill to the marrow of her bones.

'I can feel your heart kicking the palm of my hand.' The green steel of his glance plundered the heart right out of her. 'Are you nervous?'

She shook her head. She wasn't nervous of the storm, only of Lafe's closeness and her own desire to turn into his arms and feel them tight and hungry about her. She closed her eyes, ashamed of her own feelings for the man who belonged to her sister. To Gale, whom he loved, whom he understood. Lovely, tormenting Gale, who broke things when she was tired of them.

The storm vented its anger for about half an hour, then the rain began to slacken and the wind wafted a clean breath of ozone into Eden's face. Another few minutes and they were able to leave their windmill shelter. The sun sprayed out as though in apology, but by the time they reached

Bellvue they were both soaked by the tall wet grass.

Lafe marched Eden upstairs and said she was to take a hot shower and change her clothes.

'And what, pray, am I going to change into?' she asked.

'I'll find you something,' he promised.

A voluminous sweater and slacks she would look lost in, no doubt!

She luxuriated under the shower with a fat bar of soap, then rubbed herself to a glow with one of the enormous towels from the heated rail. Towel-draped, she entered the adjoining bedroom, where something shimmering and silky lay across the bed. Eden picked up the garment and found it to be a Japanese kimono. Gorgeous, with batwing sleeves intricately embroidered, and of a lovely gold colour that flared to bronze when the light shifted on the rich silk.

Eden's heart beat with excitement as she slipped into the kimono, her fingers trembled with eagerness as she tied the sash. Then she stood in front of the dressing-table mirror and studied the effect. The garment fitted her to perfection; her skin took on a creaminess against the golden silk, while her elfin hair left the collar free and upstanding.

She whistled impudently at her own reflection, whirled about as she noticed a pair of glittering objects on the rug beside the bed. She swooped on the inviting glitter and found a pair of Japanese

sandals, gold-coloured like the robe, into which her
small feet slipped easily.

So this was the outfit Lafe had rustled up for
her! Eden ran a hand down the silk, her heart
jerking in her breast when knuckles rapped the
bedroom door. She went to the door and opened it.
Donovan stood in the corridor. 'I'll take your bits
and bobs and set them to dry, miss.' He broke into
a grin as he looked her over. 'You look a proper
Madam Butterfly, if you don't mind me sayin' so,
miss.'

She grinned back at him. 'I'll get my shirt and
trews.'

She brought them to him. 'Himself says you're to
join him in the music-room for tay.' A smile played
over Donovan's knocked-about Irish face. 'I should
have put a bottle of *saki* on the tay trolley. We still
have a bottle from that trip we took to them
heathen parts a few years ago.'

'This outfit actually came from Japan?'

'Aye, miss. The collecting bug bites himself now
and again, then like as not he'll give the things
away. Play your cards right, miss, and you'll end up
takin' that fine kimono home with ye.'

Eden lost her smile. 'I shouldn't dream of angl-
ing for the kimono,' she said stiffly.

Donovan frowned down at her. 'Most of the
female clan are out to get,' he growled. 'Making
with the sweet talk, fillin' up their ditty-bags and

not carin' a tinker's curse for a man. Are ye tellin' me you're the different one?'

'I hardly think it's any of your business, Donovan!'

'Mebbe you are different from some.' His eyes narrowed meaningly. 'Himself and that sister of yours are going to fight like Kilkenny cats, for there's a devil in both of them. Stroked the right way *he* ain't so bad, but that proud beauty ain't the stroking sort.'

Donovan marched off, leaving Eden at the door of the music-room. She stared at the panelling and could not for the minute find the nerve to enter the room, to look at Lafe and realize that only a week from now she would stand in church and see him married to Gale. They would be united, and Eden's misgivings were not jealous ones. It had always been too impossible a dream to imagine him loving her ... she only wished with all her heart that Gale truly loved him.

Gareth stared when she entered the music-room. He came eagerly across to her and caught at her hands. 'You look like a lotus flower, all creamy and golden!'

'Donovan said I looked like Madam Butterfly.' She laughed and looked at Lafe. 'It's a wonderful robe. Thank you for letting me wear it while my things are dried.'

'The kimono suits you, Eden.' He spoke rather gravely. 'I should like you to keep it.'

'When would I ever wear it?' she said in confusion.

'Quite often, judging from the look on Gareth's face,' he said drily. 'Now come and hide your blush in a cup of tea.'

CHAPTER

THE hour that followed was pleasantly tense for Eden. Gareth sat on a hassock at Eden's feet, admiring her and munching cucumber sandwiches. Lafe drank several cups of tea and smoked rather a lot. The silk kimono had set him talking about the countries he had visited on business, and the shadows deepened in the room and Eden wanted this hour to go on indefinitely.

All too soon for her, he was shooting a look at his wristwatch and stubbing his cigarette. 'I'd better go and change into my evening duds.' As he climbed to his feet from the depths of an armchair, his eyes dwelt on Eden, comfortably lost in a twin chair. 'I won't rush you away if you want to stay a while longer with Gareth. I know you two haven't seen much of one another in the past week.'

'Understanding fellow,' Gareth said warmly, before Eden could speak. 'Yes, please leave Eden with me.'

Lafe strolled to the door. 'I'll tell your aunt you're with Gareth and that he'll be bringing you home, Eden.'

He was gone, firmly closing the door behind him. The room seemed to grow cold for Eden and she gave a start when Gareth caught at her hands.

He was smiling up at her and she summoned an answering smile to her lips. Lafe's cigarette smoke still lingered blue and tangy, drifting like a veil between Gareth and herself. The hands holding hers were supple and slender, without that layer of bronze, without those lingering callouses from mining and forest work.

'Lafe was smoking like a darn chimney,' Gareth remarked. 'Do you suppose he's developing a dose of pre-nuptial nerves?'

'Very likely,' Eden agreed. 'The most worldly of men aren't always proof against the approaching ordeal of a church wedding.'

'I'm darned if *we'll* have all that fuss. You don't want slipper satin, photographers and all that malarkey when we're married, do you, Eden?'

Her heart jerked into her throat, then she was saved the ordeal of betraying her dismay when Gareth turned her hands palms upwards and buried his face in them. 'Say when you'll marry me,' he pleaded. 'I—I can't think of anything but being with you, somewhere romantic, my wedding ring on your finger. Even the recital has lost all meaning for me ... your face comes drifting on to the music sheet in front of me, your voice whispers in my ear ... there's only you ... you!'

In a sort of torment he pulled her hands close against his lips, they burned and slipped to her wrist where her pulse beat so unevenly. 'Does love frighten you?' he whispered.

Love tormented her!

'It frightens me.' Gareth's eyes scanned her face in the lamplight and his eyes were dark, desiring. 'It's terrifying that one person can become one's entire world, lighting it up with a smile, plunging it into gloom with a frown.'

'Do I frown so often?' Eden attempted to speak lightly, moved by him but not so racked and stirred as he obviously was by her. She was awed that he should feel like this, and also in retreat from it. It was fastening on her, possessing her, making her feel she was under obligation to assuage it.

'You don't frown, darling,' he replied, kneeling there before her like a supplicant, 'but now and again you seem to go miles away from me. You— withdraw in spirit, and I'm lost and groping after you, wanting to touch you ... reach you.'

He reached out in this moment to touch her, and the next instant he was on his feet, jerking her up with him, pulling her into his arms. The slim, silken closeness of her seemed then to touch off something primitive in him, and her breathing turned to a gasp beneath his down-driving mouth. She struggled for a moment, then let her hands find the nape of his neck, submitting, relaxing, floating away on the wave of passion sweeping Gareth.

'You do love me!' he exulted, low and close to the life-vein in her neck. 'Oh, Eden, sometimes I've wondered ... but you couldn't lie in my arms like this, accept my kisses like this, if you didn't care.'

Eden knew otherwise.

What she felt for Lafe had made her vulnerable as never before ... this was mere physical appeasement in the warm arms of an attractive young man who cared for her.

She pulled out of his arms, stood away from him, her mouth burning against her pallor from his kisses.

Gareth ran his hand over his hair, tousled above his triumphant eyes. 'Sorry to let go like that, Eden, but that's how it is with me. I want us to be married—soon.'

'Gareth,' his name broke from her, 'p-please give me a little more time——'

His forehead contracted, the passion died in his eyes. 'Can you kiss me like that and then ask me to go on waiting for you?'

At once she was shot through with compunction, but she liked him too much to be anything but honest with him. 'Marriage is for always, Gareth, and I don't want either of us to make a mistake about—our feelings.'

'I know mine, Eden.' There was a raw edge to his voice. 'Are you saying you don't feel the same about me?'

'I—I'm fond of you——'

'Good lord, Eden, you let me near enough lose my head just now!'

She flushed. 'Do you imagine, Gareth, that women are so different from men? We're equally capable of being carried away—and I'm not totally indifferent to you.'

'But you aren't in the quagmire like I am, up to my ears in it, wanting you all the time. What do I do about it?'

They gazed at one another, the music-room silent and shadowy, then Gareth said raggedly: 'Is there someone else?'

The question shocked through her and she retreated from it, backed against the chair in which Lafe had sat smoking and talking about Japan. Her hand gripped the leather arm. 'You're the only man I go out with,' she managed.

'Right now I am, but I begin to wonder if there has been another man in your life.' Gareth's hands curled in against the sides of his slacks. 'Would it be that young doctor? Whenever we run into him you—well, you don't behave naturally with him——'

'Tony wanted Gale—not me!'

Then she bit her lip, for it sounded as if she carried a torch for Tony, who had seen only Gale and no one else. Relief stabbed as the music-room door was thrust open. Donovan stood in the aperture. 'Will you be wantin' dinner served up here or down in the dining-room?' he wanted to know.

'Downstairs, please.' Eden's silk-clad figure rustled past Gareth and he followed her moodily.

97

Lafe had left orders for Donovan to serve champagne with their meal, but it didn't succeed in adding much of a sparkle to the evening.

Gareth was quiet on the drive home, then at the gate of the Ellis house he gripped her hands and detained her. 'Don't let the things we've said tonight come between us,' he murmured. 'It's hell loving you and not having you, but I can't lose you altogether.'

'Gareth!' She drew his head down and put her lips against his cheek. 'Give me time, that's all I ask.'

She waved him off, turned slowly about and walked along the front path to the door, the fatigue of spent emotion making her feet drag. The house was silent, empty. Gale was out with Lafe. Aunt Sue and Uncle Harry were members of an old-time dancing club and they would not be home for at least another hour.

She made herself a cup of cocoa, added a couple of biscuits to the saucer and went up to bed.

Her achy, restless tiredness persisted all day Sunday, and on Monday morning she had the snuffles and was wretchedly disinclined to get out of bed. Her aunt took one look at her flushed face and hurried downstairs to phone the doctor.

But it wasn't the older Dr. Gregg who arrived an hour later, it was his son Tony. He glanced round him in a rather caged way as he stepped into the house, and Aunt Sue laid a comforting hand upon his arm. 'Gale has gone to London, my dear,' she said.

'I had to come in Dad's place, Mrs. Ellis. He's down with this summer 'flu that's going around.'

'Oh, dear,' Aunt Sue looked dismayed. 'My poor Eden has probably picked it up. She aches all over and can barely speak.'

Eden had the bug, but Tony promised he'd have her on her feet before Saturday ... the great day, as he ironically termed it.

A buzz of excitement filled the house all week, and Eden tried to feel happy about those merry sounds downstairs and what they betokened. She told herself it was the 'flu that left her feeling depressed ... with almost a sense of foreboding.

When Tony called, he said she was much better and could get up for a couple of hours. 'Poor kid, you must be fed up with being in bed with all that pre-wedding excitement going on downstairs. Postmen calling with packages. Delivery vans arriving with dress boxes ... !'

His glance strayed to a pair of plastic-swathed dresses hanging from the ledge of the wardrobe. The white dress glistened through the plastic like pristine frost, its heart-shaped bodice glittering with tiny beaded lilies, its long skirt and train like a mass of snow.

'That's quite a dress!' His smile was crooked. 'Gale will look a million in it.'

Then from her bed Eden saw his face pucker with distress. He swung to the window and stared out blindly. 'Tell me something, Eden,' he spoke roughly, 'is Gale marrying this Sheridan chap just for the luxury and high living he can give her?'

Eden winced, and then told herself that Tony had been hurt enough by disillusion. 'No woman marries entirely for those reasons, Tony. First and foremost Gale's a woman. She has to love ... and be loved in return.'

The sunshine through the window was bright on Tony's hair, but when he turned to look at Eden his eyes were sombre. 'Gale has always wanted money—she's always wanted to be someone,' he said fiercely. 'You're loyal to say she loves Sheridan, but I know, in my very soul, Eden, that she's pushing me, Sheridan and herself into a hell of heartbreak—assuming that the fellow loves her.'

'He does, Tony.' Eden felt a pain at heart that was hardly bearable. 'That's one of the tragedies of life, I think, that we must sometimes love people who can't love us in return.'

Then she changed this painful subject and asked him if it would be all right if she attended Gareth's concert in Brighton the following evening. 'We're going in Lafe's car,' Eden added when Tony looked doubtful. 'Gareth wants me to go, and I'd hate to disappoint him.'

'Another full day indoors would be Dad's recommendation, but so long as you wrap up well and don't get over-excited, then I think you should be okay.'

'How is your father, Tony?'

'Not too bad. He does rather more than he should and when he falls sick he takes a time to recover. I left him dozing in a garden chair, and he'd better still be there when I get home from my calls. By the way, I have some cream which should clear away that cold sore on your lip.' Tony rummaged about in his medical bag, but failed to find the box of cream. 'I must have left it on my desk ... anyway, I'll call back with it later on.'

'Don't put yourself out, Tony,' Eden said, aware that he had extra calls to make while his father was sick, and a heavier evening surgery to tackle.

'I can snatch half an hour to bring you the cream.' His smile was tinged with melancholy. 'Gale will want her bridesmaids looking their prettiest on Saturday.'

After Tony had left, Eden slipped out of bed and wandered to the dressing-table, where she gazed in the mirror at her peaky face. What an emotional tangle had resulted from that meeting with Lafe in the snow! If she had not stepped on that patch of ice—surely the Devil's ice—Lafe's car would have swept on its way and she would have hurried home on foot.

Eden sighed and dressed and ran a comb through her hair. She made her way downstairs, following a fragrant aroma to the kitchen, where her aunt was baking sausage rolls and apple turnovers.

'Hullo, dear.' Aunt Sue gave her niece a fond smile. 'Tony said you were getting up for a while.'

Eden lay back lazily in a kitchen rocker and let her aunt's cheerful chatter flow over her. Gale had gone up to London to attend a press conference with Lafe. It was to be televised.

'I'd die of nerves if I had to face a battery of cameras and a bombardment of questions.' Eden's aunt placed a batch of turnovers on the kitchen table and shook caster sugar over them. 'But I believe that sister of yours could face almost any situation and not bat an eyelash.'

'Gale possesses the confidence of the utterly beautiful,' Eden smiled. 'If she'd ever gone to London to work as a model, I'm sure she'd have been highly successful.'

'That glamorous creature is really as lazy as an oyster.' Aunt Sue rested her hands on her hips. Modelling for the big fashion houses is hard work, and it suited Gale to work at Monique's in town. She always modelled the smartest gowns for the more affluent customers, and had the satisfaction of knowing herself Lowton's number one glamour girl. In London she would have found more competition.'

Eden was amused by her aunt's keen summing up of Gale, who had once said with confidence to Eden that she intended to get what she wanted without joining the modelling cat race in London.

'I can hear the phone ringing in the study.' Aunt Sue broke in upon Eden's thoughts. 'Be a dear and answer it.'

It was Gareth on the line, and when he heard Eden's voice his own grew warm and eager. 'I've been terribly worried about you, darling,' he said. 'I wanted badly to come and see you, but your aunt thought I might pick up the virus and be unfit to play tomorrow evening. Are you better—will you be able to attend with the others?'

'I'm heaps better, and nothing would keep me away from the concert,' she assured him.

'That's wonderful! I know I'd play like a stick if you weren't there to cheer me on ... have you been very sick, darling?'

'I've felt a bit limp and wrung out,' she admitted. 'Have you been practising hard?'

'Like a Trojan. I not only owe it to Lafe to prove myself, but my future as a musician depends on the impression I make. *Our* future, I like to think.'

Nerves fluttered in the pit of her stomach, and then to her relief he went on to talk about Lafe's press conference at the Savoy Hotel.

'Lafe's none too keen on all that sort of thing, but it's unavoidable at times, especially now he's getting married. Actually he looks rather good on television, and your sister will probably enjoy the experience.'

Eden bit her lip, well aware that Gareth thought Gale a gold-digger. 'Are you nervous about tomorrow evening?' she asked quickly.

'I am a bit. It's a relief that you'll be there, Eden.'

'I'll be there,' she promised.

Television wasn't a popular pastime in the Ellis house. Aunt Sue preferred to knit and sew. Uncle Harry liked to settle down with a book, while Eden was bored stiff by the repeats and the juvenile brand of entertainment.

But this particular evening they all gathered round the set to watch Gale and Lafe. Eden perched herself on a hassock. Her uncle's pipe smoke drifted above her head, and she felt his hand resting lightly and fondly upon her shoulder. Aunt Sue said she hoped all the neighbours were watching!

The news began with a bank raid. Then came a political flare-up abroad, followed by a dispute at a car factory and a general walk-out.

'And now, striking a more cheerful note,' the newscaster permitted himself a smile, 'we have some film of one of industry's youngest tycoons and the lovely Cinderella whom he makes his bride this coming Saturday.'

Eden's hands locked together in her lap. The screen blurred, then she was gazing at Lafe, tall, self-assured, clad in a dark suit cut by a master hand. He smoked a cigarette in a leisurely way as he answered questions concerning his marriage and his honeymoon. Gale sat on a divan, a cool, devastating picture in the simplest of silk suits, her dark hair arranged in the Mona Lisa style that suited her so well.

When asked by a reporter if it was she who had chosen to honeymoon in the West Indies, she smiled and raised a roguish eye to his face. 'If our honeymoon plans had been left to my fiancé,' she drawled, 'we'd be honeymooning in a committee-room with a board meeting going on.'

The film sequence faded on a burst of laughter. 'Witty as well as pretty,' commented the news-caster.

Uncle Harry laughed himself as he switched off the set. Aunt Sue had bright pink cheeks. 'Gale is the limit!' she exclaimed. 'Fancy saying a thing like that—with thousands of people looking and listening!'

'Lafe appeared to enjoy the joke.' Uncle Harry gave Eden's hair a tweak. 'What do you think of your witty, pretty sister, my pet?'

Eden turned her head and smiled up at him. 'Gale could get away with anything. She looked marvellous, didn't she? So sure of herself with those lovely long legs and that seductive smile.'

'Mmm,' Uncle Harry sucked at his pipe, 'she's a stunner right enough. I'll have my agents pulling my leg in the office tomorrow.'

Within half an hour the 'stars' of that news item were sauntering into the living-room, bringing with them the glamour and gaiety of cocktails at the Savoy and sophisticated conversation. Gale had hoped to get home in time to see herself on television, and was pacified when Eden assured her that she had looked terrific.

'Your suit looked chic, and your legs were a wow. The newscaster was most impressed,' Eden added with a grin.

'What about me?' Lafe grinned, and rucked the chintz cover of the settee as he sat down, his frame having been made for something a lot larger and far less frilly. 'Don't I get a mention? I am the bridegroom-to-be.'

'You looked terrific as well.' Eden noticed that his suit, which had looked dark on television, was a warm shade of mahogany brown. The fine material sat impeccably upon his wide shoulders, while his hair held a rakish wave.

He scanned Eden on the hassock. 'You look as though you'd be easy to break in half. How do you feel, child?'

'Almost like my old self. Thank you for the delicious basket of fruit. You sent me enough to feed the street and I've lain in bed gorging myself.'

'What about the concert tomorrow evening—will you be well enough to come with us?'

'My doctor says yes. I've talked to Gareth on the phone and told him I'll be coming.'

'That made his day, hm?'

She smiled and was saved further questioning

along this line as Aunt Sue came into the room carrying a tea-tray, which she set down on the sofa table beside Lafe. He accepted a cup of tea with alacrity, also a couple of sugar-frosted turnovers. Gale went upstairs to change into something casual.

Eden sat on her hassock and hugged her knees, listening to the deep Gaelic burr of Lafe's voice as he discussed some aspect of big business with her uncle. For a short while she could enjoy his dark presence in the house, suffer secretly because he was close enough to touch ... it was wrong to feel this way about Gale's man, but how did you stop your heart from beating fast because he was near? How did you tame your feelings when the mere look of him, the mere sound of his voice made you feel you could die right now and not mind?

When Gale strolled into the room, clad in slender gold trousers and a sleeveless black top, Lafe rose to his feet. 'I've got to get some of it off hand before Saturday.'

'Poor lamb.' Gale stood in front of him and straightened his tie. 'I'll see to it that you forget all about business when I get you to those islands in the sun.'

Eden tautened on her hassock at that intimate note in her sister's voice, gripped by a primitive reluctance to hear Gale talking of the honeymoon she was so soon to share with Lafe....

'Goodnight, pixie.' He was smiling down at

Eden. 'I'll give your love to Gareth when I get home.'

'Yes, do that.' From somewhere out of her secret torment she dug up a smile, then the room was emptied of his Vulcan presence and Aunt Sue was fussing with the chintz frill of the settee.

Gale returned from bidding him goodnight. Some of her gaiety seemed switched off and she asked Eden to join her for a natter in the kitchen while she ate the meal Aunt Sue had prepared for her.

'I'm glad you're better, sweetie,' she said. 'I must admit I'm rather depending on your support on Saturday.'

Eden glanced up from the cup of tea she was pouring out. 'It's nice of you to say that, Gale.'

'We've always been together and it would have seemed—wrong, not having you with me. You're a quiet, retiring kid, but one misses you when you aren't around.'

Eden lifted her cup of tea, then put it down again, for her hand was shaking slightly. She knew why Gale was talking this way. Tony had been in and out of the house since Monday, and behind Gale's bright show of nonchalance she was beginning to feel ... afraid. Saturday was close now. Soon she would take an irrevocable step right away from the doctor's son.

'You funny kid!' Gale exclaimed. 'To your way of thinking I'm not being married on Saturday—

I'm being legally bought!'

'I suppose I'm old-fashioned in my ideas,' Eden tinkered with the tea-spoon, then she said with a rush: 'For me love comes before anything else.'

'You're tender as a spring chicken, Eden.' Gale pushed away her half touched plate and fingered her emerald and diamond ring. 'I often wish I were more like you, but I'm a realist, not a romantic. I can't see any sort of happiness for myself unless I'm surrounded by the luxurious trappings a man like Lafe can provide. I've become a spoiled cat. I must have the softest cushion and the smoothest cream— I must!'

Moodily she rose from her chair, walked to the kitchen window and frowned out upon a rather drizzly evening. Quite suddenly her slender figure stiffened. 'Tony's in the greenhouse with Uncle Harry!' she exclaimed. 'I didn't know he was coming, did you?'

'He came to bring some cream for my lip.' That bated note in Gale's voice—that *wanting* note.

'It's ages since I've talked to him.' Gale's hand clenched the curtain. 'I do believe his face looks thinner, and he's wearing that awful tweed jacket with the leather elbows!'

There was a tense silence. 'I'm going to say hullo to him!'

'No, Gale!' The words leapt from Eden's lips. 'Leave him alone! Don't go out there and rub salt in the wound you've inflicted.'

Gale swung round to Eden and she had gone pale, half-moons of shadow showing beneath her topaz eyes. 'Aren't you being rather melodramatic?' she flashed.

'You know you've hurt him.' Eden was pale herself. 'If he sees you——'

There she broke off as the kitchen door was thrust open. Tony stepped in from the garden, his hair damp and tousled, his eyes startled as they dwelt on Gale. Eden sensed his reaction acutely— the stab at the heart, the quick yearning to reach out and touch, the terrible awareness that the gulf between was too wide to be bridged by a pair of eager hands.

'Hullo, Gale!' Then he thrust a hand into his pocket and handed a small round box to Eden. 'That lip salve I promised you, Eden.'

'Thank you, Tony.' As she took the little box, she saw that Gale's eyes were signalling her to go, but she ignored the command. 'Would you like a cup of tea? It's fresh made,' she said to the young doctor.

He stood very still, as if he had not heard her, his eyes caught and held by the green and white fire of the ring on the hand Gale held to her throat. The silence stretched, grew harrowing, and it was Gale who severed it. 'The tea will stew at this rate,' she said flippantly. 'Has the cat got your tongue, Tony?'

He gazed at her beautiful, defiant face for a

moment longer, then the flare of pain in his eyes dimmed to a smoulder. 'My tongue ... and my heart,' he rejoined. 'Goodnight, Eden!'

As the door closed behind him, the sisters were left staring at one another. 'I'm tired,' Eden said at last. 'I—I think I'll go to bed.'

'Sweetie——'

- 'No, don't talk about it, Gale! It's enough that I've had to see you hurting Tony, who hasn't a spiteful bone in his body.'

'I-it was the way he looked at my ring——'

'Did you expect him to gush over it, Gale, like everyone else? He loves you, and love doesn't leave room in the heart for hand-clapping because the person you love is going to marry someone else.'

'You're talking like someone in a lovelorn magazine! If Tony's miserable then he asked for it! He refused point-blank to leave Lowton, and no man is going to tie me down in this backwoods. I—I couldn't stand it, Eden.'

'You've stood it ever since our parents died and we came here to live,' Eden reminded her. 'Lowton isn't such a bad place——'

'With love to gild the pill? What happens when the sugar wears off?'

'Need it?'

'It has no choice, my romantic little sister! Trips to the moon don't last ... the air up there is too rarefied.'

'How cynical you've become, Gale.'

'I face realities, like Lafe.' Gale found a cigarette and lit it. She began to pace the kitchen, taking restless puffs at her cigarette. 'He and I both know that love is the romantic word for desire....!'

'That isn't true!'

Gale arched an eyebrow at Eden's vehemence. 'Come, sweetie, haven't a few sessions in Gareth's arms taught you what men really want from women?'

'Desire is only half of love,' Eden argued. 'Companionship, subtle ways of understanding each other, joy in small things, strength to share sorrows, these are the other half, and when the two interlock ... well, I would call that wedlock.'

'Bully for you ... and Gareth.' Gale looked mocking. 'From the sound of that profound remark it looks as though we can soon expect an engagement announcement. Lafe will be up on stilts. His feelings for you and the young genius of the piano are quite paternal.'

'Are they?' Eden's fingers clenched on the box of cream as if they would crush it. 'I'm off to bed—I feel tired. Goodnight, Gale.'

'Eden—try to understand!'

'I understand, Gale. You want diamonds and Daimlers, not love!'

CHAPTER SEVEN

The following evening they drove to Brighton in Lafe's limousine, a smartly uniformed Donovan at the wheel.

They hoped to get to the concert hall in time to have a few words with Gareth before he began his recital, but they got held up in a traffic jam and arrived with only ten minutes to spare in which to buy programmes and get settled in their box.

'The turnout's a good one.' Gale cast an appreciative glance round the hall, fully aware that people were gazing up at her and her companions. 'Clever of you, Lafe, to arrange Gareth's recital so close to our wedding. You're a shrewd publicity man, darling.'

'I've had plenty of practice—ah, here comes our boy!'

Gareth came out on to the platform, a slim, dark-clad figure, who cast a quick glance up at their box. Eden smiled down at him and her lips formed the words. 'Good luck!' He nodded, and approached the black grand piano to a polite round of applause. He acknowledged with a grave bow, then sat down at the piano, its hood thrown back to reveal a gleaming row of keys.

Some late arrivals rustled into their seats, several

men cleared their throats, then as a waiting silence settled down over the hall, Gareth began to play.

All through the first half of Gareth's programme the audience remained strongly critical. There hung in the air the expectation of an eventual let-down. Gareth Conway was the ward of a business tycoon, so they were making it extra hard for him to prove that he was good.

Just before he was due to play the exacting and exciting *Study in C* by Rubinstein, Lafe leant forward and said quietly to Eden: 'Relax, child,' he gave her a smile. 'Gareth's keeping cool down there. He knows before the evening's over that he'll have this stiff-necked bunch begging for more.'

Lafe's confidence in Gareth was amply proved ... the silence seemed endless as the last magical notes of *Woodland Nymph* stole away, then it was broken by a thunderous wave of applause. People continued to clap, begging for more as Lafe had said they would.

At the end of the concert Gareth was beseiged in his dressing-room by people who wanted to congratulate him on his success. An executive from a recording company thrust through the crowd, demanding that Gareth lunch with him the following day. He liked *Woodland Nymph* and wanted to discuss recording terms.

At the end of a noisy half hour Gareth and his party escaped from the hall. The neon lights along the esplanade glistened on the polished bonnet of Lafe's car, and a breeze was blowing off the sea. Lafe said that his secretary had booked a table for six at Domenico's, one of Brighton's smartest restaurants, but he wanted to know if Eden felt up to the further excitement of a celebration supper.

'The evening won't be complete unless we celebrate,' she said, and felt Gareth lock an arm about her waist.

'Tony did warn you not to overtire yourself, Eden,' Aunt Sue put in rather worriedly.

There was a swish of silk as Gale swung her fur-edged stole over her shoulder. 'Don't fuss, Aunt Sue! A spot of supper won't hurt the precious infant!'

Eden's glance took in rapidly the distortion of her sister's red mouth. Yes, Gale, she thought, that's how it is! You'll feel that stab at heart each time you hear Tony's name.

When Lafe and his party walked in through the swing-doors of Domenico's, the head waiter came over, beaming 'good evening' with fulsome pleasure. He led them to a perfectly placed table, whisked a reserved card off its pristine surface, snapped his fingers for menus and the wine-waiter, and treated them as if they were royalty.

Eden saw that people at nearby tables were treating Lafe and his fiancée to stares of recognition. There was admiration in the men's eyes as Gale's stole was removed by Lafe and her shoulders creamed out of the flame silk of her gown. Aunt Sue sat gazing round the restaurant with eyes of awe, for this was the kind of place she and her husband would never have ventured into had they been dining out on their own.

Small amber lamps glowed on the tables, wine corks popped, while the blue flames beneath chafing dishes mingled with the ruby gleam of wine. Fur wraps lay across the backs of chairs and out on the dance floor women looked like costly butterflies held against the dark suiting of their partners. The atmosphere was decidedly expensive ... and then champagne arrived in a glittering ice-bucket.

Supper was delicious, needless to say, rounded off by *café brûlot* prepared at the table. Brandy was ignited in a ladle, then tipped into hot black coffee, which as the flame burned out their waiter poured into small cups, making an incense of cinnamon and cloves. An ambrosial drink which they enjoyed as they listened to the singer on the orchestra rostrum.

The song faded and Lafe drew out his cigar case. The other men declined to join him and Eden watched him kindle a Corona and puff smoke with a lazy enjoyment. 'Lafe!' Gale regarded him with exasperation. 'I wanted to dance!'

'Perhaps Gareth will give you a whirl.' He smiled shamelessly through the aromatic haze of smoke. 'I don't suppose Eden feels like being bumped about on a dance floor after her bout of 'flu.'

'Have I tired you out with my music?' Gareth studied Eden.

'Of course you haven't.' She gave his hand a reassuring squeeze. 'I love your music, but my legs are a bit woolly and I'd sooner sit and watch you dancing with Gale.'

'Come along, Liberace!' Gale switched to her feet. 'I'm too on edge to sit still, and that darned tycoon is too fond of his after-dinner cigar to let it go stale for me.'

They walked on to the dance floor and Eden smiled as she watched the shy way Gareth took hold of her glamorously gowned sister.

'How happy you must be for Gareth,' Aunt Sue said to Lafe. 'He played wonderfully well, didn't he? And everyone loved his *Woodland Nymph*. You could feel it in the air long before they began to applaud him.'

'It's a charming piece of music,' Lafe agreed. 'A woodland nymph in love, both joyous and elusive.' A screen of smoke rose up about his eyes as he spoke, and Eden felt her fingers tighten about the fluted glass that held her liqueur.

The orchestra slid smoothly into a waltz-time tune, and Eden's uncle slid back his chair and held out his hand to his wife. 'This is one of our favourites, Sue. Come along, my dear, let me give you a whirl.'

They went off to dance, leaving Eden alone with Lafe. 'That's rather a nice tune,' he said, moving round the table to a chair beside Eden's. 'Smoochy and pleasant, not battering the eardrums like a lot of the stuff they turn out these days.'

'It's an oldie.' Eden didn't dare add that the song was called *My Wonderful One*. To say those words was to voice what lay in her heart ... the secret, tormenting, guilty knowledge of what he did to her just by being beside her, tingling her nostrils with his cigar smoke, tingling her nerves when he looked at her.

'Drink your liqueur,' he ordered. 'It will put some colour in your cheeks.'

It ran along her veins like warm gold and Lafe watched insistently until the last drop was gone. 'Would you like another?'

'No, Lafe!' She caught laughingly at his arm and drew it down. 'I don't want to get tipsy. I giggle, and I'm sure you don't care for giggly females.'

'You're just a baby.' His teasing smile made her head swim as the potent liqueur hadn't. 'In your white dress, with your eyes a little heavy, you look like an infant waiting for uncle to carry you to your nursery.'

'Infant indeed!' She looked indignant. 'I bet I'm the same age as that blonde in black lace at the next table.'

He swivelled an amused green eye in the

blonde's direction. Companioned by a much older man, obviously affluent, she tensed at Lafe's appraisal and slid her gaze along the width of his shoulders. Her vermilion lips curved into a smile against her Riviera tan. 'Mmm, I like your architecture!' her smile seemed to say.

Lafe frowned and when he turned his attention back to Eden, she noticed that the irises of his eyes were glacial, his pupils sharp as jet. It gave her a jolt ... she felt that Lafe was comparing himself to the man with the blonde ... wanted not for himself by Gale but for the worldly distractions his money could provide.

'Eden,' Lafe spoke her name quietly, 'I know what you're looking unhappy about.'

'You do?' She glanced up into his face and saw his eyes lose their glitter.

'You're so young,' his strong fingers closed over her hand, resting on the table. 'You want to understand how I can enter into marriage with a woman who doesn't really love me—ah, you start, child. Did you think I didn't know? Eden, your sister has always been completely frank with me, knowing perhaps that I'd see through any pretence at passionate fondness. She has never cooed love lies in my ears ... which means she isn't like that blonde in black lace, who hasn't a thought in her head beyond getting all she can get out of one man before flitting on to the next. Girls like that make a career of acquisition. Gale wants to make a career out of being a tycoon's wife.

A smile touched Lafe's mouth, his brown hand drew Eden's into its cavernous warmth. 'Real romance might be missing from our relationship, but I'm too hardened by the years to feel the miss of it, while Gale is a gay, beautiful creature, made to be drowned in furs and to sparkle among the smart people I'm obliged to mix with and entertain in my home.'

His fingers tightened on Eden's to the point of pain. 'We're both ambitious realists ... the dreams and poetry of real romance are for the young in heart, like yourself and Gareth.'

Young in heart! A flare of denial ran through her. She felt that after his marriage she would never be young again.

He must have glimpsed in her eyes the doubts in her heart, for he said whimsically: 'It's a nice little thing you are to care about the happiness of a rough diamond like myself.'

'You aren't rough,' she protested.

He at once broke into that caustic grin that grooved his cheek deep as a scar. 'A good tailor and a capacity for absorbing knowledge do wonders,' he drawled. 'But my shaving mirror shows me twice a day that I attended the school of adversity. It's quite a place and I learned a devil of a lot as a pupil ... especially how to get on in the world, and how not to get hurt by other people.'

Lafe let go of Eden's hand and sat watching the

dancers. Then he smiled at her through the smoke of his cigar, crinkles beside his green eyes. 'Do you like secrets?' he asked.

'Of course I like them, Lafe.' Her pulses raced. 'I'm a woman, though it amuses you to call me an infant.'

'Woman ... mysterious, vulnerable, enticing ... full of mixed-up loves and hates. Frail reeds that often survive a storm while male oaks go crashing ... must I number you among them just yet, pixie?'

'Lafe, you can be exasperating! You get me all agog about a secret, then start talking to me as if I were a child.' Her brown eyes flashed, as they could at times. 'I—I know what it feels like to be a woman!'

He stared at her, and then for a long moment at Gareth with Gale in his arms. 'Of course, Eden, you are a young woman and not a charming infant.' His eyes flicked over her, and his black brows were drawn together. 'From a very reliable source I've learned that your elderly friends in the Tudor cottages are not going to be moved out of their homes after all.'

She gazed at him with a look of wonder. 'Lafe, it isn't possible!'

'According to the French, my child, it's usually the impossible that happens.' His green eyes twinkled, ice-pools with sudden sunshine spilling on to them.

Her eyes scanned his face and her heart felt that it wanted to leap with joy. 'You've had a hand in it, Lafe! I can tell—from your eyes!'

'Dangerous things, a pair of eyes,' he drawled, lifting his cigar and screening them with smoke.

'Don't tease me, tell me!' she said excitedly. 'What did you do to make the council people change their mind?'

'I bought the Banning land that was up for sale and re-sold it to the council. I took a loss on the deal on condition they sold me the site on which the cottages stand. Their tenants will have them for their lifetimes and I shall eventually build a factory on the site. With more and more people moving out of London, work is going to be needed in outlying areas, so the deal will prove a sound one in the long run.'

'Oh, Lafe!' Love drenched her heart, for she knew he had done this thing to please her. 'I was so worried about those poor old dears, and now you've set things right a-and I don't know how to thank you. For a man who calls himself hard, you're singularly generous.'

'You heard me say I'll eventually build a factory.' He spoke with a lightness belied by the sudden agitation of a nerve beside his mouth. He pressed the ball of his thumb against the nerve, but not before Eden had seen it. Tough, shrewd, the ruler of a vast commercial kingdom, yet still a man with his moments of gentleness.

'It wasn't for commercial reasons that you saved those cottages,' she said with quiet conviction.

'So I'm a rough diamond with one or two smooth facets,' he admitted with a wry smile. 'But believe me, Eden; there was a time when I strove for money alone.'

'That was understandable,' she said staunchly.

'That I, once a ragged Irish lad,' Lafe flicked his hand against his immaculate dinner-jacket, his onyx cuff-links gleaming black as his hair, 'should burn with ambition? Well, I got most of the things I ever wanted, and it doesn't hurt me to help others with my small change.'

'Lafe,' she protested, 'how cynical!'

'I am cynical, Eden. Make no mistake about it. I can do things, and face odds that would have made that ragged Irish lad weep in the clover.... !'

Came a swish of silk behind Eden, mingling with her sister's excited laughter. 'Success and champagne have gone to your feet, Gareth. I can't dance any more!'

Eden turned to look at Gareth and saw that he was boyishly flushed, his hair tousled ... but her heart was yearning over a ragged, hungry boy who had set out alone for a strange land when she was a baby. The boy—she felt certain—who still lurked in the powerful frame of the man beside her.

He got to his feet and she heard him say: 'Let us take this weary child home to her bed.'

The midnight stars blinked like sleepy eyes as

Eden tumbled into Lafe's car. Gareth was driving home in his sports car, and he bade her goodnight through the open window beside her. 'I'll see you tomorrow evening at the wedding rehearsal.' He drew the tips of her fingers to his lips. Their touch was light enough, yet she had snatched her hand away before she could stop herself.

'You runaway baby!' Gareth whispered. 'What am I to do with you?'

'Don't speed on your way home, Gareth,' she said prosaically. 'I know you're inclined to when you're driving alone.'

'Would you care if something bad happened to me?' Now his whisper had a jagged edge to it. Then he swung away from her, called goodnight to the others and lowered himself into the low-slung shape of his car. The engine gave a low whine, then almost at once he was away.

Eden let her head sink back against the soft upholstery of Lafe's car as it purred out of Brighton, leaving behind the esplanade and the lights on the water. Why was it, she wondered, that human beings were less capable than the birds and bees of managing their love life? Here was she, as emotionally tangled up as a fly in a web. There was Gale, deliberately risking her own happiness and that of two men just to satisfy an urge to be a rich, envied queen-bee, installed in a luxurious hive and fed on the honey of adulation.

When the limousine purred into the kerb in

front of the Ellis house, Eden was half asleep. She stirred when strong arms slid round her and lifted her from the car. She lay against Lafe's shoulder as he carried her indoors and lowered her to the settee in the sitting-room. She opened her eyes and brought a quizzical smile to his dark face as she said drowsily:

'Thank you, Uncle!'

The following day Eden called on her friends in the reprieved cottages. That morning they had received official notification of the change in the council's plans, and Eden found them wreathed in smiles and well aware that she had had a hand in bringing about the miracle.

It was a golden afternoon, and Eden took a glass of lemonade with Rosie in her small garden. Larks were at play in the sun-flushed sky, while the pastel confetti of Virginian stock edged the patch of grass on which Marmie was stretched out, blinking lazily, a ginger pasha of a cat.

'Bless my heart and soul!' said Rosie. 'And why should that hustling Irishman be putting himself out for the likes of a few old folk along Tiptree Lane?'

'Because he cares about people.' Eden smiled, an elfin figure perched on one of the wooden toadstools which Rosie's son had carved for her old-world garden.

'Well, it was a kind thing for him to do,' Rosie

studied her young guest, 'but most men are melting butter in the hands of a pretty female, so don't go telling me you had nothing to do with him buying these cottages.'

'I didn't deliberately set out to plead a cause,' Eden laughed. 'He wasn't going to tell me he was the purchaser until I made him tell me—he never brags about the things he does.'

' 'Tis said there's little conceit in big men and plenty of it in little ones ... my own boy was one of the big ones. Now aren't you going to eat a cake?' Rosie demanded. 'You're getting like a hairpin, you are! Look at your arms and legs!'

'I've never been voluptuous, Rosie. I take after my uncle, we're thin but wiry.'

'Put the lid on the right pot!' Rose grunted. 'You're on the fret because Gale's marrying so she'll be on velvet for the rest of her days. She's got a heart of brass!'

'Rosie——'

'Don't defend her! And I suppose the Irishman thinks she's what he needs in a wife, someone smart, slick and sassy?'

Eden nodded. 'Gale is the girl he wants ... and she made up her mind ages ago that she wanted to be rich.'

'And you like the man for himself, don't you, my girlie?' Rosie spoke with a gruff gentleness. 'Ah, well, that's the way of life. Most of us are given crosses to bear and they weigh heavy at times. But you're young, my lovely. In a few months' time the hurting won't be so bad.'

Eden avoided Rosie's eyes as she began to talk about Gareth's recital, and the glamorous restaurant where they had gone afterwards to celebrate his success. Rosie sat with an old straw hat shielding her head from the sun, her knees spread comfortably apart. Then from out of the open kitchen window came five cheerful cuckoo calls from the clock on the wall, and Eden jumped to her feet.

'I'd better be getting home,' she said. 'We're having the wedding rehearsal this evening.'

She bent over Marmie and stroked his sun-warmed belly. He purred his pleasure and seemed aware that his security was no longer threatened. 'Purr away, tiger,' Eden smiled. 'You know you're safe now, don't you?'

'Aye, he knows right enough,' Rosie agreed.

She walked with Eden to the front door of her cottage, where she suddenly cupped the girl's face in her work-hardened hands. 'Harken to me, my lovely,' she said. 'What you're feeling for Lafe Sheridan is half fascination. It's part of growing up, and you picked on him to hero-worship instead of a pop singer or an actor.'

'Yes,' Eden said, for it was easier to agree ... and there was always the hope that Rosie was right. 'I'll see you at the wedding tomorrow. Don't forget, the ceremony begins at two o'clock.'

They said goodbye and Eden walked into the town centre and made for the bus stop. She had to pass Goodall's, one of the largest stores in Lowton, and a paperback novel in the book window caught her eye. It was an army novel her uncle was keen to read, and Eden decided to dash in and buy it before the shop closed.

She darted into the big store, still quite full of shoppers despite the fact that it was almost closing time. The book department was on the fourth floor, just above the television showroom, and Eden had to use the staircase because the lift wasn't working.

A book department was like a treasure trove to Eden, and after buying the army novel, she crossed to the romantic section and took a look at the colourful display. A hovering assistant glanced at her wristwatch. It was twenty minutes past five and she was impatient to get these last-minute browsers out of her department....

Then, cutting into the silence surrounding the bookshelves, there came the frightening sound of a woman's scream. It shrilled upwards, from the television showroom below, and then a word that sounded like 'Fire!' whirled Eden from the movable rack where she was browsing. Her startled glance met that of the assistant and their eyes expressed the one thought, 'We heard wrong—it couldn't be!'

And then there arose the obvious sounds of

commotion from below ... running footsteps ... and once again that most terrifying of cries shrilled out...

'*Fire!*'

A tide of frightened people were surging down the stairs, for the lift serving this part of the store was out of order. They jostled and fought to get to safety, and Eden found herself swept along on the human tide.

The crowd seethed with body heat and fear of fire. '*Run! Run! Run!*' prodded that fear, in Eden as well as in everyone else. Being only a slightly built girl, she was jostled to the centre of the terrified crowd. Those at the rear were the most frightened because they could hear the crackle of the spreading flames and they were pushing those in front of them.

Eden stumbled down the stairs she was unable to see because of the press of people, her ankles were flayed by kicks, her sides jabbed by elbows, her mind filled with the one nightmare thought ... she must stay on her feet ... if she fell she would be trampled underfoot....

The salvation of the ground floor lay just ahead of the crowd when an elderly woman in front of Eden tottered and lost her balance. As she cried out, Eden caught wildly at her coat in an effort to save her from falling.

With safety in sight the terrified crowd surged

forward like a roaring tide to a beach, and it was then that Eden seemed to lose her precious balance. She went down under the sea of legs with the woman she had tried to help ... and then terror and pain were blotted out as a shoe struck her left temple and brought darkness.

It was a darkness that held her immobile and unknowing when her slender, trampled body was carried out of the building on a stretcher. A red blanket covered her as she was lifted into an ambulance, then the ambulance tore away from the chaotic scene outside Goodall's, away from the crowds, the fire engines, the curving jets of water and the smoke.

The accident bell of the ambulance rang imperatively as it made for the Lowton General Hospital.

CHAPTER EIGHT

THE westering sun shafted through the window of the surgical waiting-room, its ruddy glow mingling with the cigarette smoke wreathing about the dark head of the man who stood at the window. His forehead contracted as the poignant fluting of a thrush rose on the evening air, while out in the corridor there came a rattle of bottles and basins on a dressing-trolley someone was pushing.

'How much longer are the doctors going to be—oh, Harry, how much longer?' Sue Ellis gazed at her husband with distressed eyes, and with infinite gentleness he stroked the hand which he held in his.

'We must be patient, dear,' he murmured. 'Eden's in the hands of Ward Westbury and he's a fine surgeon.'

'I'll go to the canteen for some tea.' Lafe swung round from the window where the sun had just dropped out of sight. 'It's just occurred to me that I must phone the church and let the vicar know there isn't going to be a wedding rehearsal.'

He made for the door, pressing a hand down hard on Gareth's shoulder as he passed him. The boy was re-living something that had happened to him before; the interminable waiting while a sur-

geon and his team battled to keep life in a cruelly
hurt body. He had sat like this, white-faced and
shocked, the afternoon they had dragged his father
from beneath a fallen tree.

Gale sat mute by the table, lifting unseeing eyes
to Lafe when he paused beside her. 'I'll not be
more than ten minutes,' he said quietly.

The door closed behind him and again a hard,
cold tremor shook Gale. Terrible accidents happened every day, but they were bearable if they
didn't happen to people you loved ... people like
Eden ... so kind and loyal always, through everything.

It would be asking the impossible, she had once
said to Gale, to expect those you loved to be
perfect—nobody was perfect.

Not everyone like Eden tried to be as good as
possible. Good but never dull, sweet without being
cloying, and so breakable with her fine bones and
creamy skin. Now—Gale shuddered—her sister's
soft skin was marked by trampling feet, and her
cornelian eyes might never open again to smile at
those she loved.

When Lafe returned to the waiting-room carrying a tray of steaming teacups, Tony Gregg had
arrived, having got a medical friend to take over
for him at the surgery. He was sitting beside Gale
at the table, chafing her hands and talking to her in
a low-toned voice. She had relaxed a little, but
those painful tremors still shook her body every

now and again. Tony suddenly dragged off his tweed jacket and wrapped it around her. 'Let yourself cry,' he urged, when for a moment she rested her head against him. 'Don't hold back the tears.'

'This might help—a little.' Lafe handed Tony a cup of hot tea and their eyes met and held for a second or two. Lafe's eyes were startlingly green above his chalky nostrils, a nerve kicked in his dark jaw, but he left Gale where she was, resting in the curve of the young doctor's arm.

He turned away and carried a cup of tea to Gale's aunt.

'Thank you, Lafe!' She accepted the steaming cup, and for the first time she spoke his name without hesitation. 'Did you phone the vicar? Did he understand—but of course, he knows Eden, she goes with us to church every Sunday.' Aunt Sue swallowed, and then took a sip at her tea. 'What—what an unhappy wedding eve for you and Gale!'

'The vicar's informing the bridesmaids and ushers of the—rehearsal cancellation.'

His slight pause before those last words wasn't lost on Gale's uncle. He glanced up at Lafe with narrowed eyes, taking in the deep engraving of lines in the Irish face, the look of pain in the green eyes. Uncle Harry glanced away at Gale and Tony, and he understood.

'Why must misfortune strike at those who deserve it the least?' Aunt Sue's face crumpled with distress. 'It will break our hearts if we lose Eden—

she's always been such a good girl. Such a quiet, unassuming girl——'

'I know, Mrs. Ellis.' Lafe spoke deeply and quietly. 'I knew what kind of girl Eden was the evening I picked her up out of the snow.'

Half an hour later the surgeon came to the waiting-room to tell them Eden had survived her operation, but he lifted a warning hand when Aunt Sue gave a small cry of gladness. 'She is still critically ill,' he added. 'There is an injury to her spine which we dare not touch at this stage. There are indications, Mrs. Ellis, that your niece may have suffered a previous bad fall in which her back was injured—can you verify this?'

'Why, yes!' Eden's aunt clutched her husband's arm, while Gale sat rigid within the circle of Tony's arm. Lafe went tense at the window where he stood. Gareth sat forward, staring hard at Sue Ellis.

'Eden—my niece had a fall from a tree in our garden. It happened about a year ago. She was playing with Dr. Gregg's dog and it chased a cat up the tree. Eden climbed up after the cat a-and one of the branches snapped and threw her to the ground. She was badly bruised, but we didn't think at the time that—that there was any serious damage done.'

'H'm,' the surgeon massaged his chin with one of his scrubbed hands. 'Yes, that's when it would have happened—a year ago. Yes, there was damage, Mrs.

Ellis, slight enough at the time, but it has grown a little worse with each passing month. Your niece is probably an uncomplaining girl, but I would guess that in the past six months she has sustained several minor falls which she has neither mentioned to you, nor taken very much notice of herself. Each time she fell she no doubt told herself that she had tripped over something. She wouldn't take seriously her growing lack of co-ordination, for long-legged young things are clumsy. She probably called herself an idiot, jumped to her feet and walked on.'

Ward Westbury paused and glanced at each person in the waiting-room, his face sombre and his bushy brows drawn down over his keen eyes. 'For a year this young girl has stood in the shadow of a fall occurring in dangerous circumstances ... that fall occurred this afternoon when a fire broke out in the television showroom at Goodall's!'

Dusk stood in the corners of the room and silence fell upon its occupants as they thought of Eden battling all alone in the panic rush at Goodall's ... perhaps aware for the first time of the fallibility of her own legs ... suddenly aware that they were giving way beneath her ...

Gale jumped to her feet and faced the surgeon, her eyes tortured pieces of topaz set in shadowy circles, wholly concerned for someone else for the first time in her life. 'My sister is going to get well, isn't she?' A note of hysteria throbbed in her voice.

'She must! I couldn't bear it if anything happened to Eden!'

The gravity of the surgeon's face was answer enough ... Eden had a long hard pull ahead of her, dangerously complicated by the spinal condition obtained while she was shinning up a tree to help a frightened animal.

'We will do our very best for her,' he said.

'Please, let me go and see her!'

'I must warn you that she looks gravely ill, Miss Ellis——'

'I won't disturb her. I—I just want to see her.' Gale spoke with a pathetic eagerness.

'You may come as well, Mrs. Ellis.' Ward Westbury led them to the quiet room where Eden lay clinging to life. Her hair was damply tousled above her closed eyes, her lashes rested long and still upon her colourless cheeks. Beside her left temple a bruise stood out darkly.

Gale stood for long moments just gazing at her sister, then suddenly she broke down and wept ... and this for Gale was the moment when the carefully planned pattern of her life began to alter and take on a new shape.

She stumbled stricken and weeping from Eden's bedside, and out in the corridor a man stood waiting for her. He caught her in his arms and she clung to him, her mouth distorted, her tears washing the make-up from her eyes. He murmured her name, over and over, and the light of the corridor shone down on the Nordic brightness of his hair.

'W-what am I going to do?' she asked brokenly.

'You're coming with me, sweetheart. We've got to talk!'

He led her along the corridor, down a flight of stairs and out into the twilight-enshrouded grounds of the hospital. Totally absorbed in each other, they didn't notice the tall figure smoking a cigarette in the shadow of a tree ... not many paces from the slatted bench upon which Tony made Gale sit beside him.

'Gale,' he clasped her cold hands within his, 'I know this isn't the best of moments, with poor Eden so critically ill, but we haven't much time left in which to get things straight between us. My dear, can you say you don't love me? Can you marry Lafe Sheridan and cut yourself off from me for the rest of our days? *Can you?*

Her pale, distracted face was raised to his, her mascara smudged, her mouth anguished.

'Tell me to my face,' he insisted, 'that you don't love me—that you never loved me.'

'I—oh, God, you know I can't! But love has nothing to do with my marriage——'

'You're marrying Sheridan cold-bloodedly for his money?'

Gale's bowed head made reply. 'He has never asked me to love him——'

'Does he know you love me, the small town doctor who can't give you the life of luxury you think you'll be miserable without?'

'Of course he doesn't know—but everything's arranged, Tony! The wedding, the honeymoon—I can't back out, not now. He'd kill me!'

'I'd never kill for you, Gale.' Lafe loomed out of the shadows, and Gale sprang to her feet with a frightened cry. They faced one another for an emotion-charged moment, then he said: 'It's true —I never asked you to love me. We contemplated a merger—your beauty for my money—and mergers have been cancelled on the eve of the contract.'

'You mean——' she caught at his sleeve. 'You mean it's all over between us?'

'You want it to be over—and so do I.'

'I'm sorry if I've hurt you, Lafe.' She cast a look at Tony, who stood by with his hands bunched in the pockets of his slacks. Her eyes travelled over his fair, bony face and then back to Lafe. The green eyes gazing down into hers were bleak rather than angry.

'Oh, Lafe, in lots of ways you're big enough to pluck stars out of the sky for a woman, and we'd have had fun. But it isn't enough, is it? I think I began to realize it when I stood beside Eden's bed and saw her clinging to the life she's never tarnished with selfishness——'

Gale pressed a sob back into her mouth with the hand that wore Lafe's brilliant ring. 'She said weeks ago that I shouldn't marry you if I still loved Tony—and I do love him! I loved him before I ever met you, Lafe. I want to marry *him*.'

'Then so you shall.' Lafe didn't argue with her, but there was a painful twist to his mouth when he said to Tony: 'Marry her soon and make sure of her—second chances don't come to everyone.'

Gale drew off her ring and held it out to Lafe, tears rolling down her cheekbones as the moon came out and showed her a man from whose face the mask of self-possession had been stripped. He looked lost, uncertain, as though for the first time in his life he no longer knew where he was going.

'Keep it, Gale.' His voice was emptied of emotion. 'Keep all the things I ever gave you—it may be a long time before your young doctor can give you a sable coat, and I've an idea you'll never quite get over your yearning for such things.'

Then he turned and walked away ... a dark giant with smitten strength tonight.

The days that followed were melancholy ones for Eden's relatives and friends.

Gale's broken engagement received some comment in the newspapers, but local concern was centred upon Eden. She had an amazing number of friends in Lowton, made during the course of her work at the Welfare Centre.

Many kindly messages of sympathy and bunches of flowers were delivered for her at the hospital, but as yet she lay unaware of them. She lay in that limbo doctors know so much about, where even they with all their skill are sometimes powerless to intervene. The limbo between life and death, a grey land where night and day are merged together, where all forms as they move about the sickbed are wraith-like and never wholly real.

Now and again, inevitably, pain plunges the hurt body back into an awareness of life. When this happens the doctors can help and they quickly do so. Daylight and night-light gleam on the long needle of the pain-killing hypodermic. The pain ebbs away as the needle is eased gently into the thin young arm. The grey clouds enfold the tired mind and body once more ... fatigue and pain represent life ... the greyness brings peace.

For five days and six nights Eden's gallant spirit strove to stay anchored in her hurt young body, then on the sixth day her precarious grip on life began to slacken ... the nurses and doctors watched anxiously as she began to turn towards black, numbing peace like a worn-out child seeking a restful shoulder.

A summons to the hospital arrived at the Ellis house just before midnight. As the family drove quickly to the hospital, the sky let down a curtain of rain and the stars could not be seen. To Gale, gazing blindly from the window, it was as though the stars wept for her sister.

They arrived to find Eden conscious but unbearably weak, lying propped against pillows and almost as white as the sheet. Sue Ellis tried to stifle her sobs, while tears stole painfully down the face of her husband. They had loved this girl with all their hearts, for she had stepped into the shoes of the child they had lost in infancy. Now it was happening again, their dearly loved child was being taken from them a second time.

Gale moved like a ghost to her sister's bedside, where she took hold of the thin hands resting on the bedcover. The strengthless fingers curled about Gale's, while the tired brown eyes searched the mutedly-lit room ... as though for one more beloved face.

Then very slowly her glance stole down to Gale's hands, as if her fingers missed something ... the silkiness of a great green stone and the sharper feel of flashing diamonds.

'Where's your ring?' Eden whispered.

'I—I'm going to marry Tony, darling.' Gale could barely speak. 'Are you pleased?'

'Tony? Not—Lafe?'

'Not Lafe, sweetie.' Tears surged from Gale's stricken heart, rolled from her eyes, blinded her. 'You were right—I never loved him—it would have been wrong to marry him.'

'Poor Lafe!' His name sighed through Eden's lips. 'Such a lonely man!'

She began after that to drift away from a consciousness of this room, from the people who stood grieving for her. The convulsive sounds of a woman's sobs died away into another, remembered sound—that of the throbbing of a car's engine. The night-lamp grew dim, then strangely bright—the light of a car's headlamps. The white bedcover was a carpet of snow patched by pools of shadow, and Eden knew she was cold because it was a February evening with a bleak wind whistling down off the heath.

That cold wind charged along the High Street, rampant with mischief. It blew the snow in clouds about the kerbside lamps, flicked open coats and laid its touch upon quivering knees, slid beneath doorways and made the inhabitants of Lowton glad to huddle about their warm firesides.

Eden had just left work, and she smiled with delight as she ran down the steps of the Welfare Centre and saw layers of snow icing the rooftops of the houses and shops. The snowflakes were huge, scattering in the wind like feathers out of a giant pillow, and Eden had to stifle an urge to aim snowballs at a pair of bowler-hatted clerks walking in front of her.

The snow was flying hard around the corner where the shops and houses petered out into the heath, and Eden, dressed in a red coat with a pompom bobbing on her knitted cap, looked like one of those small figures inside a snowstorm paperweight as she darted across the main road.

Half blinded by the snow, she was unaware that a car had swept round suddenly from the road out of the heath. It was travelling at a rapid rate, and when Eden became aware of its bright headlamps —charging down upon her like the glaring eyes of a dragon—she broke into a run, felt ice under her feet and the next moment was skidding over. Her knees struck the wet road and her whimper of pain was lost in the scream of tyres as the big car swept dangerously close to her and skidded to a halt.

A door flew open, a large, impatiently striding figure loomed above Eden, then arms were hoisting her off the ground and she was carried to the bright headlamps of the car and subjected to the scrutiny of a pair of eyes that possessed the glacial lucidity of ice over a winter-locked lake.

Eden and the dark stranger stared at one another. Her pulses raced even faster as she recognized this man with the frosty eyes, the arching black brows and snow-tousled black hair.

'You're Lafe Sheridan!' she exclaimed, no longer aware of her stinging knees, her wet coat, or the fact that she was as helpless in his arms as an infant. This was the man she had seen on T.V. the other evening ... this was the boss of that big citrus firm ... the Irish tycoon who was in England to open several new factories.

'It's usually my firm's soft drinks that evoke the dewy-eyed appreciation,' he drawled, a quirk of a smile at the edge of his mouth.

'Sheridan's Velvet Grape is delicious,' she agreed, so intrigued by his important presence in

Lowton that she forgot her usual shyness with strangers. 'Do you invent the names of your drinks, Mr. Sheridan?'

'No, you can spare me that honour!' A long, rather sarcastic cleft slashed the hardness of his left cheek. 'Now I'm going to scold you, young lady. You should look where you're going instead of wandering across main roads in a day-dream— doubtless a dream of some blue-eyed young charmer,' he added caustically.

'I was thinking how old-world Lowton looked in the snow,' she retorted. 'I haven't got a head stuffed full of romantic nonsense.'

'Not interested in the young bloods of Lowton, eh?' His eyes glinted as they took in the snow-stung charm of her face beneath the bobble-cap. 'Are you after catching bigger game with those big brown eyes?'

Eden stiffened in his arms, then attempted a retreat from them. 'Please put me down, Mr. Sheridan. It's getting late and I have to get home.'

'Momma worries about her lamb until she's safely home in the fold, huh?'

'Really!'' Eden disliked sarcasm and in a cold voice she informed him that her parents were dead. 'And please put me down!'

He ignored the request and said coolly that he didn't believe for a moment that she was a real orphan of the storm. The effrontery of this statement left Eden speechless. This man might have the handsomest eyes she had ever looked into and a voice that pricked her skin like deep velvet, but he was most impolite!

'What possible good would it do me to tell lies about my people?' she demanded. 'What would I get out of that?'

'I could rattle off a long list of highly coloured tales that have come my way,' he smiled down caustically into her serious young face, framed against the darkness of his overcoat sleeve. 'Little Cinderellas aren't choosy about the methods they use to bag a wealthy bachelor—Lowton also has its Cinderellas, I see!'

'I'm not after your precious money!' Eden looked at him in amazed indignation. 'I think you've got a cheek to suggest it!'

He actually broke into a chuckle. 'Such sparks in those brown eyes! Aren't you going to pretend then that you find me princely and charming beneath my rugged exterior?'

Her smile stole back. 'Princely men are slender and rather fair, I think. You remind me of something carved by Epstein—you're big and cold with great empty spaces in you. And now, quite seriously, I'm going to be thought fast if you persist in holding me in your arms in the middle of Lowton's High Street.'

Their eyes met, then her lashes battered in confusion as he deliberately dropped his glance from her face and took in her helpless imprisonment in his arms. 'Lowton's one of those towns, eh? Not much entertainment, but plenty of gossip over the card tables?'

'A certain amount of gossip,' Eden admitted. 'My sister always calls it a cosy little Kremlin operating behind lace curtains.'

'So you have a sister.' He looked amused by the description.

'Yes. I'm not a fully-fledged orphan, I'm afraid. Mr. Sheridan.' Eden had caught the twitch of the lace curtains above the post-office general store, where Mrs. Turrel was in charge. Mrs. Turrel was the busiest gossip in town. 'We're not on a desert isle, you know. I—I work at the Welfare Centre, and we secretaries are expected to behave ourselves.'

He put back his black head at that and his laughter echoed along the snowy High Street and a wayward lock of hair danced in the wind above his green eyes. Then before Eden could draw breath to protest he had put her into his lavish car, swung in beside her and slammed the door. Under the overhead light his face was turned to her, boldly defined and totally unlike the faces of the men who touched her everyday life.

'I'll run you home,' he said. 'Where do you live, little chick of a secretary who must behave herself?'

For a moment she was too nervous to speak, for shut together in his car they were more alone than they had been in the tumbling snow. Here she grew tensely aware of who he was—and the way he looked. 'You were driving as though you were in a hurry to get somewhere,' she said. 'I—I don't want to take you out of your way.'

He flicked a finger at the bobble on her cap. 'Tell me where you live!'

She saw that it was useless to argue and told him how to get to the avenue where she lived. The engine sprang to life, while the pendulum of the windscreen wiper began ruthlessly to slay the snowflakes as they came dancing against the wide front window. Eden's heels sank into the fitted carpet and she gradually relaxed against the soft upholstery.

'You've gone rather quiet, little orphan,' he remarked. 'I hope I don't make you nervous?'

She dared a glance at his formidable profile and saw that the edge of his mouth was quirked on a smile. 'Do you and your sister live alone?' he asked.

Her gaze dropped to his wide shoulders. 'No, we live with an aunt and uncle. They've been like parents to us, so the Cinderella story doesn't really apply to us. Gale's beautiful.'

When Eden alighted on to the pavement in front of the Ellis house, with its snow-caked privet hedge, she found herself touching Lafe's overcoat arm. 'Come in for a cup of coffee—if you can spare the time?' she invited impulsively.

He frowned down at her, as though questioning

the motive behind her invitation.

'I make quite good coffee,' she added, a wrinkle to her nose as a snowflake touched its tip.

'Okay, lead me to it,' he said.

They crunched the snow underfoot as they walked along the front path to the door, which sheltered under a porch in which a small wrought-iron lamp glowed invitingly. The lamplight slanted down on Lafe's dark face as Eden fitted her key into the lock of the door. They entered the small, polished hall and Eden led him into the sitting-room ... where Gale stood examining a snag in one of her sheer stockings.

Eden glanced at Lafe, who was looking at her beautiful sister. 'Hullo!' Gale dropped her skirt to her knees with a husky, unembarrassed laugh. She gazed at the tall, dark stranger with topaz eyes. 'Don't tell me *you're* a clerk down at the Welfare Centre?'

Lafe murmured his name, a black eyebrow quirked.

'*The* Lafe Sheridan, the one with all the loot?'

'Yes, that one,' he drawled.

'Well, I never!' Gale gazed at him as though he had just been dropped down the chimney by an extremely benevolent Santa Claus. Eden shook the snow off her bobble-cap and explained to her sister how she and Lafe had come to meet.

'Mr. Sheridan's staying for a cup of coffee,' she added.

'Then run along and brew it, sweetie,' purred Gale. 'I'll keep Mr. Sheridan entertained.'

It was then Eden realized that she had brought more than a lonely man into the house ... she had brought in a rich one! As she paused to hang her coat in the hall she heard Gale say: 'Eden's a nice child, isn't she?'

'Is that her name—Eden?' he asked.

'Yes, we're Eden and Gale—serenity and storm.'

'Eden ... !'

The voice seemed to come from a long way off, deep, like velvet.

'Come, Eden, it isn't like you not to put up a fight. Eden, open your eyes, look at me ... you know me, don't you?'

Her eyes fluttered open and the dark face came into focus in the muted lamplight. Dark brows, green eyes, the wetness of snow on the cheekbone. 'It's snowing,' she said. 'It's cold. . . .'

Warm hands held hers, held tightly, firmly, pulling her back out of the dark peace into the white pain. 'I—I hurt my knees,' she said. 'The ice. . . .'

'I picked you up and the pain went away,' said the deep voice.

'Yes, oh, yes.' She clung to the warm hands. 'Mrs. Turrel was watching us. . . .'

'The lady in the post-office.'

'Yes. She's such a gossip, so you'd better put me down.'

'No, Eden. Stay here ... stay here, pixie. It was that bobble on your cap—it made you look like a pixie. Stay, Eden!'

'It hurts. ...'

'It won't hurt any more, I promise.'

'Dark ... on the heath. And the dragon, with green eyes....'

'Eden....'

Someone else's pain! She felt it, and her eyes opened wider, she moved her head, her hands. Pain ... but not hers!

'Darling,' said a choked voice. 'Oh, Eden!'

She saw Gale, her face wet with tears. 'Don't cry,' Eden said.

Gale put her hands over her face and the sound of her weeping filled the room.

'Don't cry!' Eden clung harder to the warm hands, her fingers felt the sinews and the callouses. 'I'll be a bridesmaid, Gale! I will!'

CHAPTER NINE

'I THINK she's waking up, Mr. Westbury!'

The white-coated figure of a man bent over Eden as she stirred; sunshine was filtering in through the window on to the fair, capped head of a nurse at the other side of the bed.

The doctor's face above Eden was fuzzy for a moment, like a face in an out-of-focus snapshot, then it gradually became more detailed, a face she had known only vaguely for interminable nights and days.

'You've had a champion sleep, haven't you?' he smiled.

'Is it morning?' she asked.

'Aye, a sunny one, the morning of August the fourth.'

'August the fourth,' she repeated after him. Then her glance was drawn to the window of her sickroom, behind which she could hear birds, lots of them. She listened wonderingly, as though to the sound of life itself. 'How they sing,' she murmured. 'Isn't it lovely?'

'There's a Scots pine almost below your window,' the doctor told her, 'and it harbours a colony of birds.'

'I always loved birds,' she said.

'I bet you did.' He spoke softly, searching the

brown eyes that seemed to fill her thin face, illuminating its pallor and its pain-haunted contours.

'I had such a strange dream last night,' she told him, trusting the rugged face with the thatch of red hair above the blue eyes. 'I dreamt that a very special friend came to see me. It was snowing in my dream.' She stared at the sunlit window. 'That's how I know it was a dream, because there was snow melting on his face.'

'It was a man, was it?' Ward Westbury smiled.

'Yes, someone I used to know.'

'A sweetheart?'

'Oh, no.' Her brown eyes grew even larger. 'I—I was never the girl he loved.'

During the days that followed Eden made steady progress, both in health and in her friendship with Ward Westbury. He was from the Midlands, a gruffly shy and brilliant man, who placed her one day in the capable, friendly hands of Cressida Moran, a young physiotherapist from America who was working in British hospitals for a year or two. She was a gay and easy person to get along with, a peach-fresh blonde whose scratched-throat voice made everything she said sound amusing.

It was Cressida's job to help Eden build up the strength in her legs, lost following the delicate operation Ward Westbury had performed on her spine. He had explained to Eden afterwards that it would take time and patience before she was fully able to walk again, and daily exercises with a physiotherapist would have to be continued even after she left the hospital and went home.

That longed-for day was drawing closer all the time ... with one shadow to mar it that was never far from Eden's thoughts.

Today was Wednesday and she had just been wheeled out into the grounds to chat with her sister Gale in the sunshine. It was a mellow September afternoon, and baby birds, late nestlings, were almost indistinguishable from the leaves that fluttered now and then from the trees. An autumnal haze drifted above the distant hills.

'It seems hardly possible that I've been in hospital so long,' Eden mused. 'So much seems to have happened....'

Her glance dwelt fondly on Gale. A melon-shaped basket bulged beside her on the bench where she sat, her glossy hair was caught back in a shoe-buckle slide, and she wore a cream pleated dress and a red jacket. A plain gold band on her left hand was companioned by a heart solitaire ... so very different from the elaborate emerald that had once glowed with each movement of her hand.

Gale's eyes followed the direction of Eden's and she touched Tony's heart-shaped diamond tenderly. 'Yes, so much has happened,' she agreed. 'You've been through hell—and I—I've found a heaven I never expected to find in Lowton of all places.'

'Marriage to Tony suits you, Gale.' Eden smiled

at the new generous fullness to Gale's mouth, the warm glow to her skin. She loved and was loved, and it showed!

At that moment a cloud moved over the sun, and Eden gave a slight shiver and clenched her hands together in her rug-covered lap. Did Lafe's clouded happiness ever haunt Gale's present radiance? It was a subject they had not fully discussed, and suddenly she said:

'Lafe must have been hurt when you said you couldn't marry him.'

Gale dug her cigarette-case out of her bag and took out a cork-tipped cigarette. She put it between her lips and as she lit it the tiny flame wavered and revealed the fact that she wasn't entirely unmoved by Eden's remark.

'He's a complex person, and a good deal of what he feels is below the surface.' Gale put back her head and sent a spiral of smoke into the air. 'He caught me with Tony the evening you were brought here, Eden. Here on this very bench where I'm sitting now. I was torn in shreds with anxiety for you ... I turned to Tony and then I knew that I couldn't go through with my marriage to Lafe.'

'You told him then how you felt?' Eden asked quietly.

'Yes. Maybe at any other time he might have cut me in two with the sharp edge of his tongue, but we were all shaken by what had happened to you, sweetie. Even Lafe was shaken! He told Tony to marry me right away. Second chances, he said, didn't come to everyone. It broke me up, the way he said it ... the way he walked off into the dark ... like a boy who was all torn inside out and who wanted to be alone with his pain.'

Eden's knuckles shone white against the plaid rug over her knees, but Gale didn't notice as she went on: 'Someone always gets hurt, but Lafe is tough. He'll forget. He will, Eden.'

'Yes.' Eden lowered her eyes in case her pain at heart was reflected in them. Three weeks ago Lafe had flown home to South Africa. He had left soon after her operation ... flying out of their lives but not out of their thoughts. Not out of Eden's. Each day, each hour, she thought of him. At the crisis of her illness he had been with her ... in a dream.

Gale brushed ash off the skirt of her dress, her white teeth troubling her lower lip. 'He wanted me to keep the presents he gave me, but it wouldn't have been fair to Tony to keep them. I'm a small town doctor's wife now, and his patients would gossip if they saw me out shopping in a sable coat.'

Eden forced a smile to her lips. 'How do you like being a housewife?'

'I'm getting used to it.' Then Gale gave a soft, almost shy laugh. 'Tony's a pet of a consolation prize, and we're beginning to make our flat look really nice. I'm longing to show you! It's quite close to the surgery and Tony's father pops in for dinner twice a week. The old darling politely assures me that he enjoys my *chili con carne* and chicken paprika, but I'll have to learn how to make a steak and kidney pie and give him a real treat.'

Eden laughed, intrigued by this new picture of Gale as an aproned housewife pottering about cooking for a husband and a father-in-law. 'Does Tony enjoy these exotic dishes you put in front of him?'

'He plies an energetic knife and fork.' Gale's eyes sparkled into Eden's, then she flipped away her cigarette stub and caught at the thin, cold hands on the plaid rug. 'I'm so thankful you're getting better. We—we all thought it was up with you—that awful night. It rained so—Lafe was soaking when he arrived. His car broke down and he couldn't get a cab. It was strange how he knew—but just after midnight he came striding in, past the Sister who tried to stop him, past everyone. *Strange.* It was almost as if his vitality poured into you and made you warm and living again—then when they said you were sleeping naturally, with even the faintest tinge of colour back in your face, he went away!

'He went quietly away, Eden. None of us noticed at the time, we were too overcome when Ward Westbury said that you had turned the corner and would get better.'

Silence between Eden and her sister, filled by the twittering of the birds in the trees. 'I thought it was a dream,' Eden said at last. 'It was the *rain* I saw on his face.'

'Yes, he was soaked. Raindrops were running down those deep grooves in his face. Eden,' Gale bent forward and kissed the thin young cheek, 'all's well, for both of us!'

Eden didn't contradict her sister, and she watched from her wheelchair as the slender figure in cream hurried away through the grounds to her brand new home and her husband.

All was well for Gale, but a tide of loneliness seemed to sweep over Eden as she sat alone in her wheelchair and pondered on the things they had talked about ... so she had not dreamed Lafe's presence at her bedside the night she had almost died. She had clung to his hands and wanted to live because he was there, holding her, willing her to live.

Now he had gone away, and his farewell to her had been a large spray of pink roses delivered by messenger, along with several expensive toys' he had obviously thought would amuse her. Swiss bonbons ingeniously packed in compartments that opened by means of a tassel. A Regency powder-box on tiny feet that tinkled a tune when the embroidered lid was raised. And to partner her blue kingfisher a translucent pink flamingo, gracefully poised for flight.

She loved them ... hated them ... wanted Lafe.

A squirrel peeped round the bole of a nearby

Scots pine, then scampered after a fallen cone with a flirt of his bushy tail. It was here that Lafe had surprised Gale with Tony ... and a few nights later he had passed with her through the darkest hour of her life. His warm, deep voice had compelled her to come back to life, and though they might never meet again in actuality, they would meet forever in her dreams.

In her dreams she would love him ... dreams would have to be enough.

Then, hearing footsteps on the path, she glanced up and saw Ward Westbury coming towards her— a stocky man, his hands thrust into the pockets of his white coat, the red hair glinting in the sunlight. He paused on the pathway in front of her wheel-chair and smiled down at her.

'It's almost teatime,' he said. 'Shall I wheel you in?'

'I'll run,' she joked.

'That will come,' he promised her, and they made small talk as he propelled her towards the hospital buildings.

'How long will it really be before I can walk again?' she asked.

A short silence followed her question as he pushed her up the ramp and through the doorway that led to the lifts. Sunlight was left behind and sudden shadow enclosed them. 'Your spinal nerves took a nasty pummelling, my lass,' he said, 'and their full functional recovery won't take place overnight. But you're a plucky one and I'm relying on you to have patience.'

'Will it be weeks—or months, Mr. Westbury?' She turned her head to look at him as he wheeled her chair into the lift and pressed for the floor on which her room was situated.

His reddish brows drew together, his blue eyes scanned her face in the rather harsh light of the lift, but it wasn't until they were in her room that he said: 'Are you worrying about getting back to your job?'

'Yes,' she admitted.

'Independent little cuss, aren't you?' He broke into a smile and wheeled her into a patch of sunlight near the window. The golden beam slanted on to the pink flamingo on her locker and the bird seemed aflame, catching and holding her gaze.

'I can't expect my people to keep me,' she replied.

Deliberately Ward Westbury bent over her, one hand holding the back of her chair. 'If you've got it into your head that you're stuck in this contraption, then get it out again! You're going to walk, in time, and I shouldn't think for a moment that those champion folks of yours worry much about the financial side of things. They're only too happy that you've—here, tell me why you're so blue this afternoon. You're usually my prize patient, the one I brag about.'

'I—I suppose I'm a little worried about going

home on Friday,' she confessed. 'It will seem like letting go of my safe towing line, for that's what you've been, Mr. Westbury.'

'You've held your chin above the waves without relying on my help all the time,' he gave her chin a light, teasing cuff. 'Mind you, I like to think my prettier patients can't get along without me, but I know you're going to.'

A ward maid came in with her tea, and Ward Westbury joined her for a quick cucumber sandwich. As they chatted he idly picked up a small, well-handled book that lay on her locker beside the flamingo. The little leather book fell open where a silk marker lay between the pages, and the surgeon scanned one of the stanzas in silence. Then he glanced up and the full impact of his shrewd blue eyes was upon Eden.

'Mackay was a passionate poet,' he murmured.

'Yes,' she said quietly.

Those blue eyes travelled over her face, took in the wide brown eyes, the slightly hollowed cheekbones, the full, sweet curve of her underlip. Then Ward Westbury glanced down again at the book in his hands. 'I'm not a reading man with much understanding of poetry,' he said, 'but there's beauty in this kind of writing—for someone who has loved—and lost.'

'I've been a fan of Eric Mackay's for a long time,' Eden's heart was beating rapidly. 'I used to read him when I was a schoolgirl and could hardly understand what he was getting at. He must have been a man of great charm to women.'

'Now I'm a bit of a boob when it comes to women,' the surgeon smiled wryly, 'until I've got them at my mercy on the operating table.'

Eden smiled and her glance rested on her companion's vital looking hair. He wasn't in the least good-looking, but in her opinion he had what it took to make him attractive to women. 'I can't believe that you haven't had your conquests, Mr. Westbury.'

His answering smile was edged with a faint melancholy. 'There was a girl—a long time ago. We were medical students together—then Margery was taken ill with polio. It struck at her lungs and she died.'

His long index finger traced the gold lettering on the fat little book of love poems. 'Even now I have trouble accepting the fact that she's dead. When she comes to me in my dreams I have to wake up to find myself alone again.'

His eyes caught Eden's before she could escape them. 'To be nourished on dreams is to go pretty hungry,' he added meaningly.

He departed in a billow of white coat, and Eden sat gazing out of the window near where she sat, not really surprised that Ward Westbury had guessed her secret. He had attended her all through her illness. There could have been times when in her pain she spoke a certain name ...

when she asked for the man who was to have married her sister!

Her breath caught on a sigh and her thoughts winged to the far-away land to which Lafe had returned. He could not bear to stay here any more. Knowing Gale, he had yet loved her, and Eden knew that life was an aching void without a certain voice to speak your name, to set your every fibre humming the secret music of love.

Her hands folded tightly about the book of love poems, and she thought of two lines written long ago by Eric Mackay:

I have been taught that happiness is coy,
And hope a moth whose wings we may destroy.

The following morning, while Cressida Moran was putting Eden through her exercises, Eden learned that the gay peach-blonde had a crush on Gareth Conway.

Eden's bedside radio was switched on, and all at once the orchestra began to play a composition of Gareth's entitled *Downland Dance*. As the small hospital room filled with the melody, Cressida's slim, strong hands paused in their manipulation of Eden's left leg.

'Gareth's music sure gets me where I breathe,' she said dreamily

Cressida was a self-assured American girl, always well groomed and giving a slight impression of toughness until you got to know her. She had admitted to Eden that she had lots of boy-friends but didn't take any of them seriously.

'I want to fall bang in love one of these days,' she had confided. 'But right now guys are just for fun. Big, huggy toys, y'know.'

Cressida hummed along with the orchestra. 'Gareth's a clever boy—and you're a lucky honey-bun.'

The smile wavered on the picador-pink lips, then Cressida briskly resumed work on Eden's legs. 'I'll soon have you sound as a roach and ready to swim off to honeymoon waters with that nice guy,' she promised. 'I guess Niagara Falls would be quite a place to visit on a honeymoon trip ... rainbows all the way. I used to love those things when I was a kid, and maybe wonder if there was a pot of gold waiting at the end of one of them.'

'Cressy, have you got Irish blood in your veins?' Eden laughed, as the slightly older girl helped her on with her tartan trews.

'Irish whimsy, huh?' Cressida broke into her scratched-throat laughter. 'I had a granddaddy who came from Ireland, if that answers your question, brown eyes.'

'It does.' With growing ease Eden swung her legs over the side of her bed and stood up with Cressida's help. A moment later she was settled in her wheelchair, her legs tingling from the massage and exercise.

'Comfortable, honey?' Cressida eased into position the small cushion that helped the slight backache from which Eden still suffered.

'Lovely,' Eden assured her. 'You're a wonderful friend, Cressy.'

'You're full of loving kindness yourself.' Cressida shot a look at her lapel watch. 'Say, I've time for a cig before I get cracking on Mrs. Gault. Join me?'

They were an American brand, and Eden remarked on their length as she accepted one.

'Everything reaches for the sky in my homeland.' Cressida held her lighter to the tip of Eden's cigarette, then she ignited her own. 'The buildings, the salami sausage, the guys. I used to go out with a ball player who stood six feet seven inches in his socks. I like tall guys, they make me feel helpless and cuddly.'

Cressida sat down on the foot of Eden's bed and crossed her long shaply legs. Her wheaten hair was arranged in a French pleat. Certainly not the helpless type, but her figure under the neat overall was shaped along cuddly lines.

'Still having butterflies about going home tomorrow?' she asked.

'One or two,' Eden admitted. 'I'm glad I shall be in your hands a while longer.'

'Sweet flatterer!'

'You're good for my morale, Cressy, as well as my legs.'

'A gal in love shouldn't need a morale booster.' Cressida studied Eden through her cigarette smoke. 'Not a gal who knows she's got the guy. You've got Gareth! He treats the rest of us like nice, homely sisters.'

Cressida spoke lightly enough, but her hazel-blue eyes had lost their carefree sparkle, and Eden wondered just how deeply Gareth attracted her ... then she gave a slight laugh when her companion said hungrily:

'By golly, do you know what I fancy right now? Salt beef between slices of rye bread, with a big spicy pickle. A dutch sweet-sour.'

'Well, I haven't any beef or pickles to offer you,' Eden smiled, 'but there's still a layer of chocolates left in that box in my locker.'

'Those luscious Swiss things?' Cressida dived for the locker, took out the circular box and popped a Sherry Soufflé between her lips. 'Mmmm, these I dig,' she purred.

'Eat all you want,' Eden invited.

'These are mighty expensive candies, honey. You won't be given another box like it in a hurry—all the same, I will have another. Apricot Mousse, I think. Mmmm, which admirer gave you these? Someone rich and fond?'

'The man my sister was going to marry,' Eden said quietly.

'The Irish tycoon? I've heard the nurses talk about him, a big, dark guy with stunning eyes, huh? That madly attractive sister of yours must have been crazy about her young doctor to give up a tycoon for him!'

'Love's more important than money, don't you think so, Cressy?'

Cressida played absently with the tassel of the chocolate box. 'Love's a funny thing. A supercolossal explosion in the heart that breaks you up and reshapes you into a whole new person. The things you want before you fall in love are never the same as the things you want after the explosion happens—or am I talking like an American movie?'

'You're talking good sense, Cressy. My sister is proof of that——' Then as Eden tautened and winced, Cressida came to her and rested a sympathetic hand on her shoulder.

'That pain in your back still troubles you, huh? A rocking-chair would help that—I've a good mind to suggest it to Red Westbury. Rocking is good therapy for a hurt back, and we should be able to find you one in this old-fashioned little town.'

'I know some people who run an antique business in Hove,' Eden spoke of the Wintons, those friends of Lafe's whom she had met at his house on the downs. 'I'll phone and ask if they can get me a rocker.'

'Good idea. Pain all gone?'

'I—it wasn't really much—I mean, compared to how it used to be.'

'It's a nerve spasm, honey. In time they'll fade away, but I'll tell Red Westbury that a rocker will help you.'

'Does he mind your nickname for him?' Eden enquired amusedly.

'Why should he? That's a nice head of hair he's got—pity, a guy like him not married. He'd make some girl a nice spouse.'

'He had a girl, but she died—and that's strictly between ourselves, Cressy.'

'So you and he exchange secrets, huh?' Cressida smiled and stubbed out her cigarette. 'I've heard that he's rather a clam about his private affairs—it must be those tiny gold lights inside your brown eyes, they're probably gamma rays against which we poor mortals have no resistance.'

'You are a fool, Cressy!'

'An Irish one! And now I'd better quit being social and cut along to Mrs. Gault. See you, brownie!'

With a wave of her hand Cressida breezed off. 'I'll send along the telephone trolley so you can phone about that rocker,' she called back over her shoulder.

Jenny Winton came to the phone, pleasantly surprised that it was Eden on the line. 'How are you, my dear?' She wanted to hear all the latest news about Eden's progress, and was certain that she could obtain her a small, comfortable rocking-chair.

There came a pause, and Eden knew that Jenny wanted to mention Lafe. Eden, fingers clenched about the telephone cord, asked if she and her husband had heard from him.

'Yes, my dear, he wrote to say there had been a dispute at one of the fruit plantations. Nothing he couldn't handle, you know Lafe. Poor man, he was so moody after his break-up with your sister, and when you're hurt and troubled it's best to plunge youself into your work. But——'

'Yes, Mrs. Winton?' Eden stared blindly at the pink flamingo which had been Lafe's parting gift.

'Between ourselves, my dear, I think Lafe needed someone with whom he could relax. It isn't easy for him, being the dynamo at the core of such a big business, and both Sam and I noticed how strained he was looking when he came to dine with us before leaving for Africa. I had the feeling ... well, to put it frankly, that he was running away.'

Oh, Lafe, Eden thought, her heart gripped by concern for him. Strong, self-controlled Lafe, running away from his lovely house on the downs; away from the little town that still held the girl who had taken his heart and then tossed it back at him.

'Are you still with me, Eden?' came Jenny's voice.

'Yes ... I was thinking about Lafe.'

'You mustn't worry about him, my dear. He'll work off the heartache, then he'll go off into the bush for some hunting.'

'You—don't think he'll ever return to England?'

'It's hardly likely. He's put in a smart managing director at the London office, and he's always happiest when he's working in the plantations. Tell me, how is Gale?'

'Happy—yes, she really is! I—I hate it that Lafe had to get hurt, but in the long run he'll be better off without a girl who—who didn't truly love him.'

'I agree, of course. Let's hope he soon meets someone who will love him as he deserves to be loved. Frankly, he's been friendly with several women, and some of them were quite genuinely fond of him, but he's the sort—oh, I don't know how to put it! One life, one love, if you get my meaning? If Gale meant that much to him, then he may never settle for less.'

These words touched Eden's heart like flashes of icy snow. She couldn't bear to think of Lafe alone, living on memories, returning home each evening to a house where a woman who loved him did not wait to greet him with a smile, a kiss.

CHAPTER TEN

GALE and her husband gave a small family party to welcome Eden home from hospital.

Eden was delighted by her sister's gay little flat. The lounge reflected Gale's very modern approach to life with its low-built furniture, tangerine carpet and gaily patterned curtains.

After dinner Eden was installed by her brother-in-law among the cushions of a half-moon couch, and Gale smiled happily as she poured coffee into little cups of unbreakable green glass. 'I like your hair in that long, tilt-ended style,' she said to Eden. 'You must keep it that way.'

'I shall until I return to work. Long hair is awkward and gets untidy when you spend the best part of the day bent over a typewriter.' Eden glanced admiringly round the lounge. 'I like this room, Gale. It's modern yet warm.'

'Our pictures are nice, aren't they?' Gale sat down beside Eden and plumped a tangerine cushion. 'We picked them up for a song while we were on honeymoon, and Tony had them framed to match the blond wood of the furniture.'

Gale's glance dwelt on her husband, and a look of wonder, almost, came into her topaz eyes. It was as though she couldn't quite believe in the happiness she had found with this quiet, slender man who would never make a big splash in the pool of life. Like his father he would want only to alleviate the aches and ills of the people of this small, pleasant town.

Tony got out the card-table and Uncle Harry sat down facing him. Aunt Sue sat with Tony's father in front of the television set. The bright curtains were pulled and they could hear autumn rain pattering against the window-panes.

'How cosy we all are!' Gale .sighed happily. 'Eden's home from that grim old hospital, and we should drink to that! Tony, open a bottle of that wine we brought back from Italy!'

'At your service, princess.' He rose from the card-table and went to the sideboard to pour the wine. He turned a moment to smile at his wife. Their eyes clung, in a way that sent shock-waves of feeling through Eden.

A little later Gale showed Eden some of her wedding presents ... among them was a beautiful set of Imari china, sent to her by Lafe.

'How kind of him.' Eden traced with her finger the intricate design on one of the plates. 'I—I wish he had come to the hospital to say goodbye to me.'

Something in Eden's voice made Gale glance up

sharply from the salad-servers she was admiring. She scanned her young sister's face, framed by the nut-brown hair that touched the shoulders of her amber dress.

Eden's heart gave a jolt ... she had almost betrayed herself!

'I always got on well with Lafe,' she forced herself to say brightly. 'I should have liked to say goodbye to him.'

'He went suddenly, without a word to anyone.' Gale sat staring at Eden. 'I hoped Gareth would come to dinner tonight. You and he—things are all right between you?'

'Of course.' Eden's hands curled together in her lap. 'He had to attend a late recording session, something to do with a technical fault on that latest record his company is putting out.'

'Gareth's right for you, Eden.'

'Yes—I know.'

'You do love him?'

'Gale——'

'Eden, there's been enough heartache! I'd hate to think that you——'

Eden's hand flew out and closed on her sister's, begging her not to say any more. 'Oh, look!' Eden broke into a smile. '*The Avengers* are coming on the box!'

Aunt Sue glanced across at Eden and said warningly: 'Half an hour of *The Avengers* and then it's home to bed for you, my dear.'

'Yes, let me have half an hour of that gorgeous MacNee man,' Eden wheedled.

When the time came to say goodnight, Gale hugged Eden rather fiercely and protectively. 'Forget Lafe!' she seemed to plead silently. 'We both know he loves *me*.'

In the days that followed Cressida Moran came each morning to the Ellis house to continue treatment on Eden's legs. Gareth was on the scene as much as possible, and it was his suggestion that the two girls spend Sunday with him at Bellevue. Cressida was off duty that day, and the weather was being genial enough for them to use the pool. A spot of swimming, Cressy said, would do wonders for Eden's leg muscles.

Eden smiled at the happy gleam of anticipation in Cressy's eyes. The thought of spending a whole day with Gareth made her look radiant.

Gareth picked Eden up in his car on Sunday morning and they drove through the sun-splashed morning towards the downs. Eden wore a pussycat bow on her dress and Gareth told her that she was looking very fetching.

'Gosh, Eden, it's grand to have you driving beside me again—I wish now that we were having this day to ourselves.'

'Gareth, you know you like Cressy! She's an extremely nice person, and very pretty.'

'H'm, I suppose she is, if you like blondes,' he

conceded. 'The trouble is, I shan't be able to make love to you with someone else looking on.'

'Gareth!'

'Don't look shocked,' he chuckled. 'Don't you realize that it's been weeks since I've really held you and kissed you properly?' And then as if this remark fired him, he drove the car into a lay-by and turned to Eden with a gleam in his eye. He took her by the wrists, and then slid his arms about her waist. 'It's been weeks,' he murmured.

She let him kiss her. Today must not be spoiled for him, but soon she was going to have to tell him that she could never marry him. Soon, but not today, not yet....

'You're trembling,' he said. 'Am I hurting you, holding you like this?'

'No, but let's drive on.'

'Poor little Eden, you've been through so much, haven't you? You look as though a touch might break you.' He kissed her cheek, then turned and took the wheel again.

As they sped along through the downs, the air was fresh and tangy, sweeping in from the sea and blowing Eden's hair back from her cheeks. The bracken had a tawny glow to it. Harebells clung to the hillocks like blue scarves, while the slow-moving sails of a windmill reminded Eden of the day she had sheltered in one with Lafe. Lightning had darted above the sails, and in her blood as she had stood within the hard circle of Lafe's arm.

'I can feel your heart kicking the palm of my hand,' he had said, unaware that it was him and not the storm that made her heart behave that way.

Gareth's car swished round into the driveway of Bellevue, disturbing the carpet of leaves lying either side of it. The house had a mellow, welcoming beauty as they came to a halt at the front of the front steps.

Donovan opened the front door. ''Tes a pleasure to see you, miss,' he smiled craggily at Eden as Gareth carried her over the threshold into the panelled hall with its beautiful chintz-panel carpet glowing underfoot.

'Hullo, Donovan!' She returned his smile. 'I thought you'd gone back to South Africa with Mr. Sheridan.'

'Aye.' Donovan spoke gloomily. 'Himself wanted me here to look out for Mr. Gareth. I misses South Africa, miss. Soon it'll be winter over here, and I hates the cold.'

'There's plenty of sunshine today,' Gareth put in. 'We're going to use the pool, Donny, but in the meantime we'll have some coffee on the sun-terrace. I've got a thirst!'

'The other young lady has arrived, and it's in the pool she is already,' Donovan grinned.

Gareth carried Eden out to the sun-terrace, which ran alongside the green-tiled pool, where Cressida was swimming about in a white swim-suit.

'Hullo there!' She pulled herself out of the water. 'I couldn't resist plunging in. It's a heavenly pool, Gareth, and the sun's really warm!'

'Our English weather goes crazy like this sometimes.' Gareth laughed and flicked a glance over Cressida's shapely figure. Her wheaten hair dripped water, her white teeth gleamed against the waterproof colouring on her lips. She looked healthy and all-American, Eden thought smilingly.

Set among tubs of tamarisk were circular rattan chairs, and Gareth settled Eden in one of these, while Cressida sprawled on a sun-mattress. Donovan wheeled out coffee and snacks, his white housecoat giving him a tropical air.

Laughter and chatter rang at the edge of the pool, the sky overhead was blue and gold. Later, when their sandwiches had settled, all three of them had a swim. Eden was more at ease in the water than on land at present, but in a while she grew tired and lay on the sun-mattress enjoying the lively antic of her two companions. They dived in and out of the water, played a game with a giant ball ... and looked in Eden's eyes so delightfully *right* together. Once when Gareth caught hold of Cressy to grapple for the blue ball, Eden saw Cressy close her eyes as though physical contact with him was unbearable pleasure.

Eden pillowed her head on her arms and knew exactly how Cressy had felt at Gareth's touch. Yet for her there was a glimmer of hope. Gareth was aware of her attraction, and he might turn to her when Eden told him that she could not marry him. A marriage built on a one-sided love could never work. She had known that all through Gale's engagement to Lafe.

The trio had luncheon in the dining-room, with its lovely antique furniture. Cressida had changed into a floral print, and her damp blonde hair was scooped back in a tortoiseshell slide.

'I can't remember ever lunching with such an edible pair of females,' Gareth remarked. 'A house is a half dead thing without any women to liven it up with their chatter and their bright dresses.'

'You say the cutest things for a British guy,' Cressida smiled, cutting her beef and changing her fork to her right hand in the American way. 'I always thought the British were reserved.'

'I had a Welsh mother and an Irish father,' Gareth informed her. 'I've also lived in Africa most of my life, in close contact with a man ... you never met my guardian, did you, Cressy? He often says things that ought to be set to music. Eden will tell you!'

Eden's lashes shielded her eyes as she ate her lunch. 'The Gaelic temperament has always been half warrior, half poet,' she agreed.

'There was trouble out on one of the plantations and he flew home to crack his boss's whip,' Gareth told Cressida.

'I hope he's coming back,' she smiled. 'I think I'd like to meet this tycoon with the velvet voice.'

'There's no telling with Lafe when he'll turn up.' Gareth shot a look at Eden and she guessed that he was thinking of Lafe's break-up with Gale. If Lafe had left this part of the world to escape from Gale, then he wouldn't be in a hurry to return.

After lunch they played records and argued amicably about their favourite recording stars. When their extremely good lunch had settled, they went out into the sunshine again.

'The tennis court's in good condition.' Gareth gave Cressy an eager look. 'If you can play in a dress——?'

'Sure I can, Garry!' Cressy answered his eager look. 'It's got a short skirt!'

'Is it okay with you, Eden, if we play?' Gareth stood holding her in his arms.

'I'll watch,' she smiled. 'I was never much good at the game, but I was always a good spectator.'

'You're a sport.' He dropped a kiss on the tip of her nose.

She lazed in a comfortable garden chair while her energetic companions enjoyed themselves out on the hard court. Cressida had a murderous left-hand service and Gareth was soon looking hot, his fair hair rumpled on his forehead.

Eden closed her eyes and dozed. The whack-whack of the tennis ball mingled with the drub-

bing of grasshoppers. Bees hummed in a nearby
rosemary bush ... she slept, and then suddenly
jerked awake as though a voice had spoken her
name.

She glanced about her, sleep-dazed, but there
was no one standing nearby. Gareth and Cressida
were over at the far side of the tennis-court, taking
a breather, yet she could have sworn that someone
had spoken. She must have been dreaming....

She turned her head, towards the trimmed hedge
with an archway in the centre of it. A tall figure
came sauntering through that archway, and Eden's
heart went into a spin. She thought for a wild
moment that she was going to pass out, for there
was no mistaking that high, wide, commanding
figure, coming across the grass towards her.

The African sun had bronzed him and his eyes
glinted like green crystal beneath black brows and
tousled black hair. He wore a loosely tailored grey-
green suit ... Lafe, a reality not a dream!

He came to her and towered over her chair.
Their eyes met. She couldn't speak or smile or do
anything. All she wanted was to fill her eyes and
her heart with the look of him.

'Hullo, Eden.' He smiled down into her eyes.
'How are you?'

Before she could catch her breath to reply to
him, a Zulu yell rang across the tennis-court. The
next moment Gareth had leapt the net and was
grabbing hold of Lafe's hand.

'You old son of a gun! Why didn't you let us know you were coming home? Gosh, it's good to see you—you've brought a nice layer of suntan with you!' The words spilled happily from Gareth. 'What do you think of Eden? She's been in the pool swimming, and soon she'll be walking again and we won't have to push her about in her pram.'

Lafe laughed, as though at a puppy who was bounding all over him. 'Simmer down, my boy,' he gave Gareth's shoulder a thump. 'Eden's looking fine. You appear to have taken a beating on the court.'

He glanced at Cressida, who was gazing at him a trifle shyly. Eden smiled to herself. Lafe had always been intimidating at first sight, a towering, black-browed figure with cool eyes that gave away no hint of the warm heart beating inside him. Eden introduced him to Cressy.

'I'm glad to know you, Miss Moran.' Lafe held out a large brown hand to Cressy. 'I won't ask if Eden's a good patient.'

Cressida smiled and shook hands with Lafe. 'She's the best, Mr. Sheridan. We all fell for her at the General, especially her surgeon, Ward Westbury.'

'Is that so?' Lafe slanted a look at Eden, and then suddenly he scooped her slight figure up in his arms and carried her to the sun-terrace. She felt her heart beating very fast and hoped he couldn't feel it.

'You look different,' he said. 'Now let me see—why, it's your hair! It's grown long and you've lost your pixie look.'

'I suppose you're sorry about that?' Her arms lay round his neck as he carried her, and she was close, drowning in those crystal-green eyes.

His quirk of a smile was familiar and dear. 'Everything going all right, Eden? No complications to set you back?'

'None, thank goodness. Mr. Westbury doesn't want me to rush things, but I do get impatient at times ... to stand on my own two feet again.'

'Ward Westbury did a wonderful job on you, Eden. By Christmas you'll be walking in the snow again.'

She nodded, but couldn't speak. How wonderful to walk with him in the snow again, but this was just a flying visit. He would be gone again by the time the rooftops were white and she wore again her winter cap with the bobble on the top.

'Surprised to see me back in England?' he asked.

'I'm glad to see you back.' She tilted her chin. 'Will you be staying long?'

'Who knows?' His eyes flickered over her face and they held the strangest expression. '"*They change their sky, not their soul, who run beyond the sea,*"' he quoted.

Lafe lowered her into one of the terrace chairs. 'We'll throw a party, Gareth,' he said. 'If I remember rightly it's Eden's birthday this month. Which day is it, Eden?'

'The twenty-eighth, but I don't want to put you to the bother of a party——'

'It will be no bother,' he assured her. 'We'll invite your people and all your friends and have a cake baked with rosebuds on it.'

Her people ... Gale....

Eden accepted a glass of lemonade from Gareth, and she stared into it as she listened to the deep rumble of Lafe's voice. He was talking to Cressida about her work, one long leg crossed upon the other, Turkish cigarette smoke drifting from his lips.

'Have things quietened down at the Pretoria plant?' Gareth asked him.

'Yes, that was why I was able to fly over for a visit. How are things with you, Gareth?'

The sun burned out in the western sky as they talked, dusk crept through the garden and brought an autumnal chill with it. As they went indoors for dinner, the whistling of a lonely redbreast followed them.

A strange kind of week followed for Eden.

'Why did he have to come back?' Gale demanded. 'He's made everyone feel restless again—like the north wind blowing!'

'He won't be staying,' Eden assured her, trying to close her mind to what Lafe had said about not being able to change his soul because he changed his sky. He meant that once again—just once—he had to see the girl he loved.

Eden hated to be inactive and she persuaded her uncle to let her help with some of the work he brought home from the office. She was in his study on Friday afternoon, deep in columns of figures, when Gareth called on her.

He came to tell her that a concert tour through North America had been arranged for him ... and he wanted Eden to go with him as his wife.

He sat on a corner of her uncle's desk and gazed at her persuasively. 'Please say you'll marry me and you'll come,' he said. 'You're almost back on your feet, darling, and I'll take the greatest care of you.'

She looked at him and gathered the nerve for what she had to say in reply. 'I'm sorry, Gareth,' she spoke gently. 'I'm very fond of you, but I don't believe in half-and-half marriages.'

'You mean,' he thrust a lock of hair back from his sorrel eyes, 'you're saying you don't—care enough?'

'Not enough to marry you, Gareth.'

'Eden, I'd be very good to you—I'd make you love me!'

'Love can't be forced, my dear,' she said wisely. 'It's either there in your heart, or it isn't. And I want you to be loved—you're too fine a person to be wasted on less than the real, overwhelming thing.'

Silence hung between them, then he carried her hand to his lips and gently kissed her fingers. 'Trying to catch you, Eden, has been like trying to capture a butterfly in a net. Someone else has always stood between us—no, sweetheart, I'm not asking you to tell me who he is, but I know he exists. I know also that he belongs to another woman.'

She could not control the nervous jump of her hand in his. It gave her away to him, irrevocably, and clouded his sorrel eyes. His eyes dwelt on her thin heart of a face, slipped to her tremulous mouth. 'I shan't forget you in a hurry,' he said. 'You'll always be my woodland nymph.'

Aunt Sue came in with tea and toasted scones on a tray, eager to be told a pleasant and expected piece of news. They had to disappoint her. Gareth drank a quick cup of tea, then loped out to his sleek racing car and drove rapidly away.

'He's such a nice boy,' Aunt Sue murmured, distressed.

'Too nice to be married for companionship alone, Aunt Sue.'

Her aunt nodded. 'With Gale happily settled down, I want the same for you, my dear. Gareth seemed so right for you, but it wouldn't work if you don't care sufficiently for him.'

'It wouldn't be fair—you always said that about Gale when she meant to marry Lafe.'

'Yes, Eden. I said it, and I meant it—why, I

wonder, did Lafe return?' Aunt Sue's eyes dwelt broodingly on her niece. 'Why didn't he stay away? He can only be hurt by seeing Gale again.'

Eden bent quickly over her interrupted work, and she didn't look up again until she heard the study door close behind her aunt. There were tears in her eyes when she looked up. They blinded her, and then fell on to her cheeks.

She had longed to see him, but now ... now she wished that she might never see him again. It hurt too much, this heart full of love she could give to no other man.

On Friday evenings Aunt Sue and Uncle Harry went to their old-time dancing club. Tonight the club was holding a competition to find its best pair of dancers, and Eden had insisted that they go as usual. She would be all right. She didn't mind being alone for a few hours.

Her aunt and uncle left for the dance looking a charming couple in their evening clothes. 'Bring home that dancing trophy!' Eden called out after them.

'We'll do our best,' laughed her uncle.

'And not be late, dear,' sang out her aunt.

The front door closed behind them. Their car swished away in the wind and rain that had set in. Raindrops fell down the chimney of the sitting-room fire and sizzled as they met the flames.

Eden was deep in a book when the doorbell

suddenly pealed through the house. She glanced up, frowning, for she wasn't expecting a caller. Then her teeth bit down hard on her bottom lip in case Gareth had called back to pressure her into marrying him ...

Again there was a long peal on the doorbell. Whoever was calling could see the light through the sitting-room window, and the person was not going away until she answered the door. She pushed herself to her feet, for she could now walk far enough to make it to the front door. By the time she got there she was panting with the effort, and her legs almost buckled under her when she opened the door and found herself face to face with Lafe.

She clung to the door, staring at his dark face, his rain-plastered hair, then he swept in, his arms took her up against his motoring jacket, the door slammed behind him.

In the sitting-room he put her into a chair, then stood above her rather grimly, a nerve kicking in his jaw.

'What's the matter, Lafe?' She found her voice at last. 'You look terribly worried——'

He gnawed his lip, then dragged off his jacket and tossed it to one side. 'It's pelting with rain.' His glance swept round the room and settled on the sideboard with its glasses and a pair of decanters. 'May I pour a drink?' he asked.

'Of course.'

'You must join me, Eden.' He stepped to the sideboard and poured whisky into a couple of glasses, adding water to one of them. Eden gazed at him, her heart thumping with a strange apprehension. Something was wrong ... she could tell from the nervous way he handled the decanters.

Her eyes scanned his grim face as he came to her and placed a drink in her hand. 'Lafe, what's wrong?' she demanded.

'I——' He tossed back the whisky in his own glass. 'I don't like breaking bad news to people over the phone—the fact is, Eden, young Gareth's had an accident in his car!'

'Oh, no!'

'He skidded on the wet road, about half a mile from Bellevue—he has concussion and a fractured leg. They took him to the Lowton General—I've just come from there.'

Eden stared at Lafe in a daze, then she began to tremble, and Lafe put an arm around her and made her drink her whisky. 'I'm sorry, Eden,' he murmured. 'I know it's a blow, but they assured me at the hospital that he's going to be all right.'

'I—it's all my fault,' she whispered.

'No, Eden! How can it be your fault?'

'I—I told him today that I couldn't marry him. He was upset when he left me——'

Lafe's whisky glass rang on the surface of the settee table. 'You told him *what*?'

'I—I'm sorry, Lafe. I know that like everyone

else,' tears started to her eyes, she choked out the words. 'I know you wanted me to marry Gareth—but I don't love him! I couldn't marry him, not loving him——'

Lafe's hands cupped Eden's face, tipped it to him. His face had a curious paleness under the suntan, and her tears ran down over his hands.

'It's my fault Gareth's hurt——' Her face, all wet with tears, crushed itself against Lafe's shoulder. His hands tightened on her, holding her there against him. 'Don't cry,' he pleaded. 'My poor child, you've been through too much—and now this! Naturally you aren't ready yet to marry Gareth——'

'Don't!' Tormentedly she wrenched away from him. 'I'm not a child who doesn't know her own heart! I know it too well! I'd run from it if I could, but you said yourself that you can't run away from your own soul!'

She gazed up at him, he stared down at her. The clock ticked, the rain beat at the windows, the heavens roared with thunder....

'Eden....' Her name came from his as a murmur in a dream.

Only a second more, only a heartbeat, then suddenly she was crushed in his arms. For a wild second she fought him ... then she melted into him like moonlight into snow.

She couldn't think ... she didn't want to ... why ask now why he kissed her? All that mattered was that he kissed her....

Then he had torn away from her. He breathed unsteadily and thrust the rain-tousled hair back from his forehead. 'I had no right to do that,' he groaned. 'You're upset and I——'

'Why did you kiss me, Lafe?' The question broke from her and she felt she would die if his kisses had meant that he was just sorry for and had no other way to comfort her.

'A man has these moments of madness—I'm sorry, Eden.'

A moment of madness! She swayed as though he had struck her, then the next instant was caught and held by him, and as if that touch was not to be borne she struggled with him, broke away from him, and then lost all strength in her legs and crumpled to the floor.

'*Eden!*' He was on his knees beside her, cradling her, crushing his lips to hers. 'Eden, darling—darling——'

'Lafe——' She touched his black hair with her hands, touched his face, felt the wetness of a tear on his cheekbone. 'Lafe, my dearest,' she sighed.

'Sweet, foolish child.' He groaned the words. 'This is just madness on your part.'

'Sweet madness,' she whispered. 'Let me enjoy it, let me pretend that it's *me* you kiss, that it's *me* you want.'

'Pretend?' He held her away from him, his hands buried deep in her hair, holding her so that her hair streamed over his arm. 'Pretend I care for for *you*?'

'I—I know it's really Gale you want——'

'My God!' He lifted her to her feet and his eyes were green and dangerous as they caught hers and held them. 'I had no youth to match with yours, no more innocence, that was why it was easy to marry Gale! You—from the moment we met in the snow I wanted never to let you out of my arms. A child, with great brown eyes and lips no man had kissed. My child, I'm holding you now, but in the end I shall have to let you go.'

'No!' She clung to him. 'Oh, no, not if you love me, Lafe!'

'I'm too old for you, little one. Too hard and worldly.'

'Lafe,' she touched his tousled hair and smiled, 'there's a lonely Irish boy inside you and I love him so much that I hurt with it. You came back, Lafe. I thought you came back to see Gale once more. If you came back to see me—if you love me—then don't leave me all alone again.'

'Have I been trying to be too noble?' he murmured, the tenderest of smiles softening his face.

'Much too noble!'

'I heard you tell Gale—at Bellevue it was—that you cared for Gareth.'

'I said it to save my foolish pride,' she confessed. 'She came close to guessing how I felt about you, so I used Gareth as my shield. He's such a dear—I never meant to hurt him.'

'The accident wasn't your fault, my darling.' Lafe kissed away the anxious frown that creased her forehead. 'The car skidded, and as luck would have it his leg was hurt and not one of his arms. A fractured arm could have affected his playing.'

'I hope he's put in Cressy's charge,' Eden said, a smile of complicity forming on her lips. Then her eyes found Lafe's face and she asked a heart-felt question: 'Didn't you ever love Gale?'

'I was lonely, Eden, and such men are not always wise. I'm happy that in the end we both came to our senses and called a halt to a marriage that would have been empty for both of us.'

'Yet she said that the evening you became engaged, you looked at her....' Eden's fingers clenched on his lapel. 'She told me you cared for her.'

'Perhaps she looked a little like you that evening and I made believe that I had you ... Eden, do you understand the meaning of the love of a mature man?'

She felt the pain of his grip and her cornelian eyes held a sudden radiance as they met his. 'I'm not an infant, Lafe. I never was. I love you, and I want to be loved by you....'

She got no further. He gathered her close to him and everything was lost in his kiss ... all the pain, leaving only the promise of an abiding love.

Harlequin Presents..

Three of the world's greatest romance authors.
Don't miss any of this new series. Only 75c each!

ANNE HAMPSON

☐ #1 GATES OF STEEL
☐ #2 MASTER OF MOONROCK
☐ #7 DEAR STRANGER
☐ #10 WAVES OF FIRE
☐ #13 A KISS FROM SATAN
☐ #16 WINGS OF NIGHT

☐ #19 SOUTH OF MANDRAKI
☐ #22 THE HAWK AND THE DOVE
☐ #25 BY FOUNTAINS WILD
☐ #28 DARK AVENGER
☐ #31 BLUE HILLS OF SINTRA
☐ #34 STORMY THE WAY

ANNE MATHER

☐ #3 SWEET REVENGE
☐ #4 THE PLEASURE & THE PAIN
☐ #8 THE SANCHEZ TRADITION
☐ #11 WHO RIDES THE TIGER
☐ #14 STORM IN A RAIN BARREL
☐ #17 LIVING WITH ADAM

☐ #20 A DISTANT SOUND OF
       THUNDER
☐ #23 THE LEGEND OF LEXANDROS
☐ #26 DARK ENEMY
☐ #29 MONKSHOOD
☐ #32 JAKE HOWARD'S WIFE
☐ #35 SEEN BY CANDLELIGHT

VIOLET WINSPEAR

☐ #5 DEVIL IN A SILVER ROOM
☐ #6 THE HONEY IS BITTER
☐ #9 WIFE WITHOUT KISSES
☐ #12 DRAGON BAY
☐ #15 THE LITTLE NOBODY
☐ #18 THE KISSES AND THE WINE

☐ #21 THE UNWILLING BRIDE
☐ #24 PILGRIM'S CASTLE
☐ #27 HOUSE OF STRANGERS
☐ #30 BRIDE OF LUCIFER
☐ #33 FORBIDDEN RAPTURE
☐ #36 LOVE'S PRISONER

N 402 P